Daniil Kharms was born in 1905. In the 1920s, Kharms was active in the Association of Real Art, a group whose absurdist writings caught the attention of the Soviet censors. Kharms was first arrested in 1931–2 and as a result he could only publish writing for children. By the end of the decade, even these writings were considered unfit for publication and in 1941 Kharms was re-arrested and died, probably in a Leningrad prison hospital, early in 1942.

INCIDENCES

DANIIL KHARMS

Edited and translated, and with a new
postscript by Neil Cornwell

Introduced by Simon McBurney

A catalogue record for this book is
available from the British Library on request.

The right of Daniil Kharms to be identified as the author
of this work has been asserted in accordance with
the Copyright, Designs and Patents Act 1988

Neil Cornwell's translations of a number of the stories included here
have previously appeared in *The Plummeting Old Women and Other Stories*,
Lilliput Press, Dublin, 1989

The translation of 'Yelizaveta Bam' first appeared in *Daniil Kharms and
the Poetics of the Absurd*, edited by Neil Cornwell, Macmillan Press, 1991

First published in 1993 by Serpent's Tail

First published in this five-star edition in 2006
by Serpent's Tail, 4 Blackstock Mews, London N4 2BT
www.serpentstail.com

ISBN: 1-85242-480-X
ISBN-13: 978-1-85242-480-0

Printed by Mackays of Chatham

10 9 8 7 6 5 4 3 2 1

Contents

This one has chickens in it :)

Introduction
by Simon McBurney

My palms are sweaty. I watch nervously as the audience rock with laughter at the reader before the reader before me. I applaud enthusiastically hoping it will remove some of the tension. The next reader is even more gripping and amusing. Now it's my turn. Suddenly I am up on stage. I open the pages of Daniil Kharms and look out into the dark mass that is the audience.

– Read fast and loud.

That was my instruction from Neil Bartlett, the director of the evening to celebrate 20 years of Serpent's Tail publishing house. I open the pages in front of me and wonder if anyone in the audience will get what I get about Daniil Kharms.

And I am even sweatier now, three months later in 105 degrees of heat here in Los Angeles. July, 2006. The air conditioning in the car does not work. With one hand I try to hold onto the flapping map; the other grips the wheel. For a moment the wind means I am driving blind. Swerving from the oncoming traffic, I start shouting at everything. Further from the world of Kharms than it is possible to be, I wonder if the night of the Serpent's Tail reading will help me write something lucid about a man whose writing deconstructs the rational, ruptures our expectations and collapses meaning for fun. I can't think of it now but I am sure it will come to me when I get to the hotel. Is it for fun? Why did Kharms write as he did? And what is there to say about it anyway in July 2006 in Los Angeles, for god's sake?

1985. Moscow, in a hot little room with the radiators roaring, was when I first heard of him. Through the double panes of glass, snow had gathered on the lower edge. Outside the Moscow street was dark, only a feeble street light on the snow held tight by 25 degrees of frost.

I am there with my mother. Visiting my brother Gerard, who is studying music. The room is stuffed with people, musicians, writers, artists, and friends. It is the third apartment we have been to today. In each one, despite the difficulty of obtaining provisions at that time, tables groan with food and vodka glasses are pressed into our hands. After the first visit the sub-zero temperatures do not register at all. A sudden burst of laughter distracts me. I turn back to my brother by the table loaded with pickled herring and Poltava sausage.

– What are they talking about?

– Telling a story.

– What about?

– About a man who had nothing.

– Eh?

– Well he was a red-headed man but he did not have any hair so he was only called red-headed hypothetically. My brother begins to giggle mischievously.

– Eh?

– Kharms, he says. The writer. He is called Daniil Kharms.

– Never heard of him.

– Not published. People just remember his stuff. It was illegal to publish him. Too dangerous. In fact it was an incredible chance that his writing has survived at all.

– How come?

– Well the story goes like this.

In the early days of the siege of Leningrad, a German bomb fell on a block of flats in Mayakovsky Street. 1942. One side of the building was destroyed. On the other side still standing, many flats have their windows blown in. In one of these, on the fourth floor, a young man and a young woman were scrabbling around trying to gather from amongst the fragments of shattered glass and plaster a mass of scattered notebooks, sheets of paper, books and personal possessions.

What they were saving was the life's work of a young man who has been arrested only six weeks or so before. His real name was Daniil Ivanovitch Iuvachov... He called himself Kharms. Almost nothing of what he wrote was published in his lifetime. Only a close circle of friends knew his work, many of them also writers...

– Very dangerous man, says my brother, with a glint in his eye. Stalin liquidated him in 1942.

– For what.

– For writing things like... *On one occasion a man went off to work and on the way he met another man who, having bought a loaf of Polish bread, was wending his way home.*

– *And that's just about all there is to it.*

He translates this to his friends who roar their approval and talk about Kharms til three in the morning. Gradually I piece a picture together. He wrote jokes. As well as poems, playlets, short stories and philosophy. Sometimes in tiny fragments or episodes. Incidents he called them. Though these writings might just as well have been called happenings, even just... things.

'Things' taking place in Leningrad. The scenes are set in Soviet flats with people eating pickled herring and Poltava sausage, in rooms with paper-thin walls where anyone can hear anything, flats with communal corridors, collective kitchens, shared bathrooms and spying concierges. The hero of 'The Old Woman' listens to the engine driver Matvie Filippovich coming home and desperately tries to stuff the dead old woman into his suitcase so no one will see. He then agonisingly attempts to pretend all is fine as he passes through the kitchen past the suspicious and devious Mar'ia Vasil'evna on his way to the toilet.

Eventually he escapes into streets seething with people trying to buy food and scrape a living, filling the pavements and over-crowding the tramcars. A place where people take the same path to work throughout their lives, blindly repeating their mechanical actions of existence, reiterating the same words, in an absurd and endless chain of predictable, prosaic existence. These events of everyday urban living, Kharms' raw material, are drawn from the physical reality of the city. His city. Post-revolutionary St Petersburg.

And what makes Kharms' vision special is the way he trans-forms these events. A man who has the same dream of policemen over and over (The Dream: Incident 12) cannot wake up and becomes so thin he is thought unhygienic and thrown out with the rubbish. Another man going out to buy sausage, loses every-thing he has, breaks his glasses and then dreams he is brushing his teeth with a candlestick (Losses: Incident 16). The repetition of life becomes ludicrous. Old women who lean out of windows plummet out one after the other relentlessly (The Plummeting Old Women: 3). Pushkin and Gogol pratfall over one another in perpetual motion (Pushkin and Gogol: 7). Two men continually beat the shit out of each other again and again, it seems forever. (The Story of the Fighting Men: 11).

Kharms' 'things' were never written down but transmitted orally, taking on a mythic status. They exploded the boring minu-tiae of ordinary life into vast incomprehensible flashes of the eternal. People told them to each other as jokes for laughter. As parables for grasping the absurdity of their lives. They told them for comfort. They told them as prophecies. They told them as signs of mutual understanding that nothing written should be believed, and that language itself should not be trusted, except as music that can provoke laughter and offer consolation.

His world is a world out of human control, but none the less created by the human will. The megalopolis. The image embraced by Joseph Roth in the pitiless '30s Paris of *The Legend of the Holy Drinker*, or the labyrinthine Buenos Aires of Jorge Luis Borges, or the city of evil in Meyehold's *The Bed Bug*.

A blaring horn reminds me of the megalopolis I am in. Completely seized up in traffic for mile after mile I am streaming with sweat and desperate to reach the safety and sanity of my hotel. The heat fuels my frustration and fury and I turn up the radio for some soothing music. The people in the next car turn up theirs. A man wheeling a supermarket trolley with his whole life contained within it shakes a fist at me. Luckily there is Tom Waits to save me.

'Heart attack and Vine… At heart attack and Viiiiiiiiine…' He wails as we pass Vine Avenue.

Kharms sets his fantastic stories in streets his audience knows, shops they used, in houses they recognised. Having tried to deal with the dead old woman, the 'hero' walks out onto Nevsky Prospect, buys beer on Fontanka Street, and is assaulted on the corner of Liteinaya Street. These were as familiar as Oxford Street, Eight Avenue, Sunset Boulevard or the Champs Elysée. But on these familiar streets the protagonists are assaulted, are unable to buy what they want, fall out of windows, cannot bury the ashes of their husbands, are unable to perform on stage because they keep on throwing up… No one seems to understand what the other is saying. They speak at cross purposes, frequently getting the wrong end of the stick or repeating things compulsively like absurd meaningless mantras. Kharms has been called an 'absurdist'. And Russians point out that he lived in a society that offered much to be absurd about. But the absurdity he describes is not just Russian, it is universal.

I finally get to the hotel. There is a queue. Behind the cashier is a glass box. In it reclines a semi-clad young woman sleeping with a book over her head. I am so astonished that the receptionist has to ask me three times who I am before I can reply. Desperate for a coffee I scuttle to the restaurant.

    – Coffee please?

    – What kind? Oh, what are you reading?

    – Coffee please?

    – What's the script?

    – Sorry?

    – I'm an actor too, what's it about? asks the waiter. I hand him Kharms.

    – It's…er…funny.

    – A comedy, huh? Who's directing?

    – Short stories, I mumble.

    – Cool, he says, wanna eat? He puts down the book and begins to recite a list of specials. All I can see is his mouth. His words convey no meaning to my mind whatsoever. The list is endless.

    – Excuse me… I say and rush from my table. All I want is coffee…

I go to my room in a fury and try to write. Blimey, I think, I need Kharms now like I need a hole in the head. The air conditioning is working now but too well. Within minutes I am shivering as if in a deep freeze. I decide to go for a walk. After five minutes it is too hot to walk and I burn the bald patch on the top of my head. Maybe I am only going bald hypothetically, I tell myself. Back in my room I try to sleep but cannot because I am jet-lagged. And so I pace up and down with fury and start yelling the text aloud. Very loud. Louder and louder as I did, as I was told to, on the night celebrating Serpent's Tail's twentieth anniversary. Then I remember. That is when they started laughing.

Read 'Pakin and Rakukin' (Incident 30) if you do not believe me. Read it loudly and aggressively to friends, particularly children. Set in some minor bureaucratic office is the story of Pakin bullying the 'snottering' Rakukin to death. Very cruel, the laughter it provokes is a laughter that reveals. Cuts open. We all recognise human brutality, and our own pitiless capacity for violence. It is absurd, unpleasant but utterly recognisable. But then being laughed at in real life is not pleasant either. It reveals a truth we would rather not have exposed. And as this particular story shows, Kharms is a master of cutting open, but he is also a master of turning corners. From the brutal and uproarious death of Rakukin and Pakin's hilariously callous and disgruntled response comes, unexpectedly and shockingly, this strange ending in which Rakukin's soul suddenly crawls out of his body and

> ...the tall figure of the angel of death came out from
> behind the cupboard and, taking Rakukin's soul by the
> hand, led it away somewhere, straight through houses
> and walls. Rakukin's soul ran after the angel of death,
> constantly glancing malevolently back. But then the
> angel of death stepped up the pace and Rakukin's soul,
> leaping and stumbling, disappeared into the space
> beyond the turning-point.

This extraordinary change is a total surprise. The hilarious modulates into the numinous. And this shock, this mystical jolt, is part of Kharms too. The story becomes a poem, the joke becomes a prediction. Look closely and you will see this everywhere in his work. At the end of 'The Young Man who Astonished a Watchman' (14) the young man disappears to heaven leaving behind a smell of burnt feathers. The hero of 'The Old Woman' at its climax falls to his knees in front of a caterpillar and prays 'In the name of the father, the son and the holy ghost'; in 'I had Raised Dust' at the end of this dream of a desperate running to escape, quite suddenly 'a mighty relaxation…' stops his heart. Over and over again in his plays, in his stories and his poems he seems to see his own fate and the destiny of those around him.

On 2 February 1942, a few months after his wife Marina Malich and his friend the philosopher Yakuv Druskin, had rescued his works from the bombed-out flat in Mayakovsky Street, Daniil Kharms died. No one knows exactly how or where he died, but probably of starvation in a prison hospital only a few streets from his home, while the German bombs rained on the frozen city in the first bitter winter of the siege.

So, if anyone asks you about Kharms, read these pieces aloud. Preferably read them to children of any age from six to 60. Read loud and fast. Then you too will hear. You will hear his ear. The music, not just the laughter of those listening, nor just the conjunction of the language from the brilliantly silly to the brutally bloody, but you will hear, underneath all of this, the bass note which is the foundation of this work. What you will hear is a shout. Like the man in 'They Call Me the Capuchin' who 'when walking on the street I always take with me a thick knotty stick… in order to batter any infants who get under my feet… But just you wai,t you swine, I'll skin your ears yet!' You will hear Kharms himself emitting an exuberant shout of fury and delight. He shouts furiously, hilariously, at the ridiculous, at the chaotic, the brutal, and the despotic, and grasping delight in the incomprehensible, unknowable, unquantifiable energy of life; energy that will be there long after tyrants fall and the consequences of their abominations end. No one has ever written such a shout in such a way ever before. It is the dangerous and joyous shout of defiance. A visionary yell. A shout of hope and consolation. Read and rejoice.

THE OLD WOMAN

A Tale

... And between them the following conversation takes place.

Hamsun

In the courtyard an old woman is standing and holding a clock in her hands. I walk through, past the old woman, stop and ask her: – What time is it?

– Have a look – the old woman says to me.

I look and see that there are no hands on the clock.

– There are no hands here – I say.

The old woman looks at the clock face and tells me: – It's now a quarter to three.

– Oh, so that's what it is. Thank you very much – I say and go on.

The old woman shouts something after me but I walk on without looking round. I go out on to the street and walk on the sunny side. The spring sun is very pleasant. I walk on, screwing up my eyes and smoking my pipe. On the corner of Sadovaya I happen to run into Sakerdon Mikhailovich. We say hello, stop and talk for a long time. I get fed up with standing on the street and I invite Sakerdon Mikhailovich into a cellar bar. We drink vodka, eat hard-boiled eggs and sprats and then say goodbye, and I walk on alone.

At this point I remember that I had forgotten to turn off the electric oven at home. This is very annoying. I turn round and walk home. The day had started so well and this was the first misfortune. I ought not to have taken to the street.

I get home, take off my jacket, take my watch out of my waistcoat pocket and hang it on a nail; then I lock the door and lie down on the couch. I shall recline and try to get to sleep.

The offensive shouting of urchins can be heard from the street. I lie there, thinking up various means of execution for them. My favourite one is to infect them all with tetanus so that they suddenly stop moving. Their parents can drag them all home. They will lie in their beds unable even to eat, because their mouths won't open. They will be fed artificially. After a week the tetanus can pass off, but the children will be so feeble that they will have to lie in their beds for a whole month. Then they will gradually start to recover but I shall infect them with a second dose of tetanus and they will all croak.

I lie on the couch with my eyes open and I can't get to sleep. I remember the old woman with the clock whom I saw today in the yard and feel pleased that there were no hands on her clock. Only the other day in the second-hand shop I saw a revolting kitchen clock and its hands were made in the form of a knife and fork.

Oh, my God! I still haven't turned off the electric oven! I jump up and turn it off, and then I lie down again on the couch and try to get to sleep. I close my eyes. I don't feel sleepy. The spring sun is shining in through the window, straight on to me. I start to feel hot. I get up and sit down in the armchair by the window.

Now I feel sleepy but I am not going to sleep. I get hold of a piece of paper and a pen and I am going to write. I feel within me a terrible power. I thought it all over as long ago as yesterday. It will be the story about a miracle worker who is living in our time and who doesn't work any miracles. He knows that he is a miracle worker and that he can perform any miracle, but he doesn't do so. He is thrown out of his flat and he knows that he only has to wave a finger and the flat will remain his, but he doesn't do this; he submissively moves out of the flat and lives out of town in a shed. He is capable of turning this shed into a fine brick house, but he doesn't do this; he carries on living in the shed and eventually dies, without having done a single miracle in the whole of his life.

I just sit and rub my hands with glee. Sakerdon Mikhailovich will burst with envy. He thinks that I am beyond writing anything of genius. Now then, now then, to work! Away with any kind of sleep and laziness! I shall write for eighteen hours straight off!

I am shaking all over with impatience. I am not able to think out what has to be done: I needed to take a pen and a piece of paper, but I grabbed various objects, not at all those that I needed. I ran about the room: from the window to the table, from the table to the oven, from the oven again to the table, then to the divan and again to the window. I was gasping from the flame which was ablaze in my breast. It's only five o'clock now. The whole day is ahead, and the evening, and all night is . . .

I stand in the middle of the room. Whatever am I thinking of? Why, it's already twenty past five. I must write. I move the table towards the window and sit down at it. A sheet of squared paper is in front of me, in my hand is a pen.

My heart is still beating too fast and my hand is shaking. I wait, so as to calm down a little. I put down my pen and fill my pipe. The sun is shining right in my eyes; I squint and light up my pipe.

And now a crow flies past the window. I look out of the window on to the street and see a man with an artificial leg walking along the pavement. He is knocking loudly with his leg and his stick.

– So – I say to myself, continuing to look out of the window.

The sun is hiding behind a chimney of the building opposite. The shadow of the chimney runs along the roof, flies across the street and falls on my face. I should take advantage of this shadow and write a few words about the miracle worker. I grab the pen and write: 'The miracle worker was on the tall side.'

Nothing more can I write. I sit on until I start feeling hungry. Then I get up and go over to the cupboard where I keep my provisions; I rummage there but find nothing. A lump of sugar and nothing more.

Someone is knocking at the door.

– Who's there?

No one answers me. I open the door and see before me the old woman who in the morning had been standing in the yard with the clock. I am very surprised and cannot say anything.

– So, here I am – says the old woman and comes into my room.

I stand by the door and don't know what to do: should I chase the old woman out or, on the contrary, suggest that she sit down? But the old woman goes of her own accord over to my armchair beside the window and sits down in it.

– Close the door and lock it – the old woman tells me.

I close and lock the door.

– Kneel – says the old woman.

And I get down on my knees.

But at this point I begin to realize the full absurdity of my position. Why am I kneeling in front of some old woman? And, indeed, why is this old woman in my room and sitting in my favourite armchair? Why hadn't I chased this old woman out?

— Now, listen here — I say — what right have you to give the orders in my room, and, what's more, boss me about? I have no wish at all to be kneeling.

— And you don't have to — says the old woman. — Now you must lie down on your stomach and bury your face in the floor.

I carried out her bidding straight away . . .

I see before me accurately traced squares. Discomfort in my shoulder and in my right hip forces me to change position. I had been lying face down and now, with great difficulty, I get up on to my knees. All my limbs have gone numb and will scarcely bend. I look round and see myself in my own room, kneeling in the middle of the floor. My consciousness and memory are slowly returning to me. I look round the room once more and see that it looks as though someone is sitting in the armchair by the window. It's not very light in the room, because it must be the white nights now. I peer attentively. Good Lord! Is it really that old woman, still sitting in my armchair? I crane my neck round and have a look. Yes, of course, it's the old woman sitting there and her head's drooped on to her chest. She must have fallen asleep.

I pick myself up and hobble over towards her. The old woman's head is drooping down on to her chest; her arms are hanging down the sides of the armchair. I feel like grabbing hold of this old woman and shoving her out of the door.

— Listen — I say — you are in my room. I need to work. I am asking you to leave.

The old woman doesn't budge. I bend over and look the old woman in the face. Her mouth is half open and from her mouth protrudes a displaced set of dentures. And suddenly it all becomes clear to me: the old woman has died.

A terrible feeling of annoyance comes over me. What did she die in my room for? I can't stand dead people. And now, having to mess about with this carrion, having to go and talk to the caretaker and the house manager, to explain to them why this old woman was found in my place. I looked at the old woman with hatred. But perhaps she wasn't dead, after all? I feel her forehead. Her forehead is cold. Her hand also. Now what am I supposed to do?

I light up my pipe and sit down on the couch. A mindless fury is rising up in me.

– What a swine! – I say out loud.

The dead old woman is sitting in my armchair, like a sack. Her teeth are sticking out of her mouth. She looks like a dead horse.

– What a revolting spectacle – I say, but I can't cover the old woman with a newspaper, because anything might go on under the newspaper.

Movement could be heard through the wall: it's my neighbour getting up, the engine driver. I've quite enough on my plate without him getting wind that I've got a dead old woman in my room! I listen closely to my neighbour's footsteps. Why is he so slow? It's half-past five already! It's high time he went off. My God! He's making a cup of tea! I can hear the noise of the primus through the wall. Oh, I wish that blasted engine driver would hurry up and go!

I pull my legs up on to the couch and lie there. Eight minutes go by, but my neighbour's tea is still not ready and the primus is making a noise. I close my eyes and doze.

I dream that my neighbour has gone out and I, together with him, go out on to the staircase and I slam the door behind me on its spring lock. I haven't got the key and I can't get back into the flat. I shall have to knock and wake up the rest of the tenants and that is not a good thing at all. I am standing on the landing thinking what to do and suddenly I see that I have no hands. I incline my head, so as to get a better look to see whether I have any hands, and I see that on one side, instead of a hand, a knife is sticking out and, on the other side, a fork.

– So – I am saying to Sakerdon Mikhailovich, who for some reason is sitting there on a folding chair – So, do you see – I say to him – the sort of hands I have?

But Sakerdon Mikhailovich sits there in silence and I can see that this is not the real Sakerdon Mikhailovich, but a clay version.

At this point I wake up and immediately realize that I am lying in my room on the couch and that by the window, in the armchair, sits a dead old woman.

I quickly turn my head in her direction. The old woman is not in the armchair. I gaze at the empty armchair and I am filled with a wild joy. So, that means all this was a dream. Except, where did it start? Did an old woman come into my room yesterday? Perhaps that was a dream as well? I came back yesterday because I had forgotten to turn off the electric oven. But perhaps that was a dream as well? In any case, it's marvellous that I don't have a dead old woman in my room and that means I won't have to go to the house manager and bother about the corpse!

But still, how long had I been asleep? I looked at my watch: half-past nine; it must be morning.

Good Lord! The things that can happen in dreams!

I lowered my legs from the couch, intending to stand up, and suddenly caught sight of the dead old woman, lying on the floor behind the table, beside the armchair. She was lying face up and her dentures, which had jumped out of her mouth, had one tooth digging into the old woman's nostril. Her arms were tucked under her torso and were not visible and from under her disordered skirt protruded bony legs in white, dirty woollen stockings.

— What a swine! — I shouted and, running over to the old woman, kicked her on the chin.

The set of dentures flew off into the corner. I wanted to kick the old woman again, but was afraid that marks would remain on her body and that subsequently it might be decided that it was I who had killed her.

I moved away from the old woman, sat down on the couch and lit my pipe. Thus twenty minutes went by. Now it had become clear to me that, come what may, the matter would be put in the hands of a criminal investigation and that in the bungling which would follow I would be accused of murder. The situation was turning out to be serious, and then there was that kick as well.

I went over to the old woman again, leaned over and started to examine her face. There was a small dark bruise on her chin. No, nothing much could be made of that. What of it? Perhaps the old woman had bumped into something when she was still alive? I calm down a little and begin pacing the room, smoking my pipe and ruminating over my situation.

I pace up and down the room and start feeling a greater and greater hunger. I even start shaking from hunger. Once more I rummage in the cupboard where my provisions are kept, but I find nothing, except a lump of sugar.

I pull out my wallet and count my money. Eleven roubles. That means I can buy myself some ham sausage and bread and still have enough for tobacco.

I adjust my tie, which had got disarranged in the night, pick up my watch, put on my jacket, go out into the corridor, painstakingly lock the door of my room, put the key in my pocket and go out on to the street. Before anything else I have to eat something; then my thoughts will be clearer and then I'll do something about this carrion.

On the way to the shop, I keep on thinking: shouldn't I go

and see Sakerdon Mikhailovich and tell him all about it and perhaps together we could soon think out what to do. But I turn this idea down on the spot, because there are some things which one has to do alone, without witnesses.

There was no ham sausage in the shop and I bought myself half a kilo of saveloys. There was no tobacco, either. From the shop I went to the bakery.

There were a lot of people in the bakery and there was a long queue waiting at the cash desk. I immediately frowned but still joined the queue. The queue moved very slowly and then stopped moving altogether, because some sort of a row had broken out at the cash desk.

I pretended not to notice anything and stared at the back of a nice young lady who was standing in the queue in front of me. The young lady was obviously very inquisitive: she was craning her neck first to the right and then to the left and she kept standing on tiptoe, so as to get a better view of what was happening at the cash desk. Eventually she turned round to me and said: – You don't know what's going on there, do you?

– I'm afraid I don't – I answered as drily as possible.

The young lady twisted herself from side to side and finally again addressed me: – You wouldn't like to go up there and find out what's happening, would you?

– I'm afraid it doesn't concern me in the slightest – I said, even more drily.

– What do you mean, it doesn't concern you? – exclaimed the young lady – you are being held up in the queue yourself because of it, aren't you?

I made no reply and merely bowed slightly. The young lady looked at me with great attention.

– Of course, it's not a man's job to queue for bread – she said. – I'm sorry for you, having to stand here. You must be a bachelor?

– Yes, I am a bachelor – I replied, somewhat taken aback, but automatically continuing to answer somewhat drily, with a slight bow at the same time.

The young lady again looked me up and down and suddenly, touching me on the sleeve, she said: – Let me get you what you need and you can wait for me outside.

This threw me completely.

– Thank you – I said. – It's extremely kind of you but, really, I could do it myself.

– No, no – said the young lady – you go outside. What were you intending to buy?

– Well, then – I said – I was intending to buy half a kilo of black bread, only of the round sort, the cheapest one. I prefer it.

– Right, well that's fine – said the young lady. – So, go on, then. I'll buy it and we can settle up afterwards.

And she even gave me a slight shove under the elbow.

I went out of the bakery and stood right by the door. The spring sun is shining right in my eyes. I light up my pipe. What a delightful young lady! It's so rare these days. I stand there, my eyes screwed up from the sun, smoking my pipe and thinking about the delightful young lady. She has bright brown eyes, too. She's simply irresistibly pretty!

– Do you smoke a pipe? – I hear a voice beside me. The delightful young lady hands me the bread.

– Oh, I'm forever grateful to you – I say, taking the bread.

– And you smoke a pipe! I really like that – says the delightful young lady.

And between us the following conversation takes place.

She: So, you buy bread yourself?

I: Not only bread; I buy everything for myself.

She: And where do you have lunch?

I: Usually I cook my own lunch. But sometimes I eat in the bar.

She: Do you like beer, then?

I: No, I prefer vodka.

She: I like vodka, too.

I: You like vodka? That's wonderful! I'd like to have a drink with you sometime.

She: And I'd like to drink vodka with you, too.

I: Forgive me, but may I ask you something?

She: (*blushing furiously*) Of course, just ask.

I: All right then, I will. Do you believe in God?

She: (*surprised*) In God? Yes, of course.

I: And what would you say to us buying some vodka now and going to my place? I live very near here.

She: (*perkily*) Well, why not, it's fine by me!

I: Then let's go.

We go into a shop and I buy half a litre of vodka. I have no more money left, except a bit of change. We talk about various things all the time and suddenly I remember that in my room on the floor there is a dead old woman.

I look round at my new acquaintance: she's standing by the counter and looking at jars of jam. I gingerly make off towards the door and slide out of the shop. It just happens that a tram is stopping opposite the shop. I jump on the tram, without even looking to see what number it is. I get off at Mikhailovskaya Street and walk to Sakerdon Mikhailovich's. I am carrying a bottle of vodka, saveloys and bread.

Sakerdon Mikhailovich opened the door to me himself. He was wearing his dressing-gown, with nothing on underneath, his Russian boots with the tops cut off and his fur hat with the earflaps, but the earflaps were turned up and tied in a bow on top.

– Jolly good – said Sakerdon Mikhailovich on seeing that it was me.

– I'm not dragging you away from your work? – I asked.

— No, no — said Sakerdon Mikhailovich. — I wasn't doing anything, I was just sitting on the floor.

— Well, you see — I said to Sakerdon Mikhailovich — I've popped round to you with vodka and a bite to eat. If you've no objection, let's have a drink.

— Fine — said Sakerdon Mikhailovich. — Come in.

We sent through to his room. I opened the bottle of vodka and Sakerdon Mikhailovich put two glasses and a plate of boiled meat on the table.

— I've got some saveloys here — I said. — So, how shall we eat them: raw, or shall we boil them?

— We'll put them on to boil — said Sakerdon Mikhailovich — and while they're cooking we'll drink vodka with the boiled meat. It's from a stew, it's first-class boiled meat!

Sakerdon Mikhailovich put a saucepan on to heat, on his kerosene stove, and we sat down to the vodka.

— Drinking vodka's good for you — said Sakerdon Mikhailovich, filling the glasses. — Mechnikov wrote that vodka's better than bread, and bread is only straw which rots in our bellies.

— Your health! — said I, clinking glasses with Sakerdon Mikhailovich.

We drank, taking the cold meat as a snack.

— It's good — said Sakerdon Mikhailovich.

But at that moment something in the room gave out a sharp crack.

— What's that? — I asked.

We sat in silence and listened. Suddenly there was another crack. Sakerdon Mikhailovich jumped up from his chair and, running up to the window, tore down the curtain.

— What are you doing? — I exclaimed.

But Sakerdon Mikhailovich didn't answer me; he rushed over to the kerosene stove, grabbed hold of the saucepan with the curtain and placed it on the floor.

– Devil take it! – said Sakerdon Mikhailovich. – I forgot to put water in the saucepan and the saucepan's an enamel one, and now the enamel's come off.

– Oh, I see – I said, nodding.

We sat down again at the table.

– Oh, to the devil with it – said Sakerdon Mikhailovich – we'll eat the saveloys raw.

– I'm starving – I said.

– Help yourself – said Sakerdon Mikhailovich, pushing the saveloys over to me.

– The last time I ate was yesterday, in the cellar bar with you, and since then I haven't eaten a thing – I said.

– Yeh, yeh – said Sakerdon Mikhailovich.

– I was writing all the time – said I.

– Bloody hell! – exclaimed Sakerdon Mikhailovich in an exaggerated tone. – It's a great thing to see a genius before one.

– I should think so! – said I.

– Did you get much done? – asked Sakerdon Mikhailovich.

– Yes – said I. – I got through a mass of paper.

– To the genius of our day – said Sakerdon Mikhailovich, lifting his glass.

We drank. Sakerdon Mikhailovich ate boiled meat and I . . . the saveloys. Having eaten four saveloys, I lit my pipe and said:

– You know, I came to see you, to escape from persecution.

– Who was persecuting you? – asked Sakerdon Mikhailovich.

– A lady – I said.

But as Sakerdon Mikhailovich didn't ask me anything and only poured vodka into his glass in silence, I went on: – I met her in the bakery and immediately fell in love.

– Is she attractive? – asked Sakerdon Mikhailovich.

– Yes – said I – just my type.

We drank and I continued: – She agreed to go to my place and drink vodka. We went into a shop, but I had to make a run for it out of the shop, on the quiet.

– Didn't you have enough money? – asked Sakerdon Mikhailovich.

– No, I had just enough money – I said – but I remembered that I couldn't let her into my room.

– What, do you mean you had another woman in your room? – asked Sakerdon Mikhailovich.

– Yes, if you like, there's another woman in my room – I said, with a smile. – Now I can't let anyone into my room.

– Get married. Then you can invite me to the reception – said Sakerdon Mikhailovich.

– No – I said – snorting with laughter. – I'm not going to get married to this woman.

– Well then, marry that one from the bakery – said Sakerdon Mikhailovich.

– Why are you so keen to marry me off? – said I.

– So, what then? – said Sakerdon Mikhailovich, filling the glasses. – Here's to your conquests!

We drank. Clearly, the vodka was starting to have its effect on us. Sakerdon Mikhailovich took off his fur hat with the earflaps and slung it on to the bed. I got up and paced around the room, already experiencing a certain amount of head-spinning.

– How do you feel about the dead? – I asked Sakerdon Mikhailovich.

– Completely negatively – said Sakerdon Mikhailovich. – I'm afraid of them.

– Yes, I can't stand dead people either – I said. – Give me a dead person and, assuming he's not a relative of mine, I would be bound to boot him one.

– You shouldn't kick corpses – said Sakerdon Mikhailovich.

– I would give him a good booting, right in the chops – said I. – I can't stand dead people or children.

– Yes, children are vile – agreed Sakerdon Mikhailovich.

– But which do you think are worse: the dead or children? – I asked.

– Children are perhaps worse, they get in our way more often. The dead at least don't burst into our lives – said Sakerdon Mikhailovich.

– They do burst in! – I shouted and immediately stopped speaking.

Sakerdon Mikhailovich looked at me attentively.

– Do you want some more vodka? – he asked.

– No – I said, but, recollecting myself, I added: – No, thank you, I don't want any more.

I came over and sat down again at the table. For a while we are silent.

– I want to ask you – I say finally. – Do you believe in God?

A transverse wrinkle appears on Sakerdon Mikhailovich's brow and he says: – There is such a thing as bad form. It's bad form to ask someone to lend you fifty roubles if you have noticed him just putting two hundred in his pocket. It's his business to give you the money or to refuse; and the most convenient and agreeable means of refusal is to lie, saying that he hasn't got the money. But you have seen that that person does have the money and thereby you have deprived him of the possibility of simply and agreeably refusing. You have deprived him of the right of choice and that is a dirty trick. It's bad form and quite tactless. And asking a person: 'Do you believe in God?' – that also is tactless and bad form.

– Well – said I – I see nothing in common there.

– And I am making no comparisons – said Sakerdon Mikhailovich.

– Well, all right, then – I said – let's leave it. Just excuse me for putting such an indecent and tactless question.

– That's all right – said Sakerdon Mikhailovich. – I merely refused to answer you.

– I wouldn't have answered either – said I – except that it would've been for a different reason.

– And what would that be? – asked Sakerdon Mikhailovich limply.

– You see – I said – in my view there are no believers or non-believers. There are only those who wish to believe and those who wish not to believe.

– So, those who wish not to believe already believe in something? – said Sakerdon Mikhailovich. – And those who wish to believe already, in advance, don't believe in anything?

– Perhaps that's the way it is – I said. – I don't know.

– And in what do they believe or not believe? In God? – asked Sakerdon Mikhailovich.

– No – I said – in immortality.

– Then why did you ask me whether I believe in God?

– Simply because asking: 'Do you believe in immortality?' sounds rather stupid – I said to Sakerdon Mikhailovich and stood up.

– What, are you going? – Sakerdon Mikhailovich asked me.

– Yes – I said – it's time I was going.

– And what about the vodka? – said Sakerdon Mikhailovich. – There's a glass each left, you know.

– Well, let's drink it, then – I said.

We drank down the vodka and finished off the remains of the boiled meat.

– And now I must go – I said.

– Goodbye – said Sakerdon Mikhailovich, accompanying me across the kitchen and out to the stairway. – Thanks for bringing the refreshments.

– Thank you – I said. – Goodbye.

And I left.

Remaining on his own, Sakerdon Mikhailovich cleared the table, shoved the empty vodka bottle on top of the cupboard, put his fur cap with the earflaps on again and sat down on the floor under the window. Sakerdon Mikhailovich put his hands behind his back and they could not be seen. And from his disordered dressing-gown protruded his bare, bony legs, shod in Russian boots with the tops cut off.

I walked along Nevsky Prospect, weighed down by my own thoughts. I'll now have to go to the house manager and tell him everything. And having dealt with the old woman, I shall stand for entire days by the bakery, until I encounter that delightful young lady. Indeed, I have remained in her debt for the bread, to the tune of forty-eight kopecks. I have a fine pretext for seeking her out. The vodka I had drunk was still continuing to have its effect and it seemed as though everything was shaping up very nicely and straightforwardly.

On Fontanka I went over to a stall and, on the strength of my remaining change, I downed a big mug of kvass. The kvass was of poor quality and sour, and I walked on with a revolting taste in my mouth.

On the corner of Liteinaya some drunk or other staggered up and pushed me. It's a good thing I don't have a revolver: I would have killed him right here on the spot.

I walked all the way home, no doubt with a face distorted with malice. In any event, almost everyone I passed swung round to look at me.

I went into the house manager's office. At the table sat a short, dirty, snub-nosed, one-eyed, tow-headed female and, looking into her make-up mirror, she was daubing herself with lipstick.

– And where's the house manager? – I asked.

The girl remained silent, continuing to daub her lips.

– Where's the house manager? – I repeated in a sharp voice.

– He'll be here tomorrow, not today – replied the dirty, snub-nosed, one-eyed and tow-haired female.

I went out on to the street. On the opposite side, an invalid was walking along on an artificial leg and knocking loudly with his leg and his stick. Six urchins were running behind the invalid, mimicking his gait.

I turned into my main entrance and began to go up the stairway. On the first floor I stopped; a repulsive thought had entered my head: of course, the old woman must have started to decompose. I had not shut the windows, and they say that with an open window the dead decompose all the quicker. What utter stupidity! And that devil of a house manager won't be there until tomorrow! I stood in indecision for several minutes and then began to ascend further.

I stopped again beside the door to my flat. Perhaps I should go to the bakery and wait there for the delightful young lady? I could try imploring her to let me in to her place for two or three nights. But at this point I recollect that she has already bought her bread today and so she won't be coming to the bakery. And in any case nothing would have come of it.

I unlocked the door and went into the corridor. At the end of the corridor a light was on and Mar'ia Vasil'evna, holding some rag or other in her hands, was rubbing it over with another rag. Upon seeing me, Mar'ia Vasil'evna cried: – Some auld man was asking for ye!

– What old man? – I asked.

– I don't know – replied Mar'ia Vasil'evna.

– When was that? – I asked.

– Don't know that, either – said Mar'ia Vasil'evna.

– Did you talk to the old man? – I asked Mar'ia Vasil'evna.

– I did – replied Mar'ia Vasil'evna.

– So, how come you don't know when it was? – said I.

– Twa oors ago – said Mar'ia Vasil'evna.

– And what did this old man look like? – I asked.

– Don't know that, either – said Mar'ia Vasil'evna and went off to the kitchen.

I went over to my room.

– Suppose – I thought – the old woman has disappeared. I shall go into my room, and there's no old woman there. Oh, my God! Do miracles really not happen?!

I unlocked the door and started to open it slowly. Perhaps it only seemed that way, but the sickly smell of decomposition in progress hit me in the face. I looked in through the half-open door and, for a instant, froze on the spot. The old woman was on all fours, crawling slowly over to meet me.

I slammed the door with a yelp, turned the key and leapt across to the wall opposite.

Mar'ia Vasil'evna appeared in the corridor.

– Were ye calling me? – she asked.

I was so shaken that I couldn't reply and just shook my head negatively. Mar'ia Vasil'evna came a bit nearer.

– Ye were talking to someone – she said.

I again shook my head.

– Madman – said Mar'ia Vasil'evna and she again went off to the kitchen, looking round at me several times on the way.

– I can't just stand here. I can't just stand here – I repeated to myself. This phrase had formed somewhere within me. I kept reiterating it until it reached my consciousness.

– No, I can't just stand here – I said to myself, but carried on standing there, as though paralysed. Something horrific had happened, but there was now the prospect of dealing with something that perhaps was even more horrific than what had already occurred. My thoughts were spinning in a vortex and I could see only the malicious eyes of the dead old woman, slowly crawling towards me on all fours.

Burst into the room and smash the old woman's skull in! That's what needs to be done! I even gave the place the once-over and was relieved to see a croquet mallet which, for some unknown reason, had been standing in the corner of the corridor for many a year. Grab the mallet, burst into the room and bang . . . !

My shivering had not passed off. I was standing with my shoulders arched from an inner cold. My thoughts were jumping and jumbled, backtracking to their point of departure and again jumping ahead and taking over new spheres, and I stood, lending an ear to my own thoughts, and remaining as though to one side of them, as though not their controller.

– The dead – my own thoughts explained to me – are a category to be reckoned with. A lot of use calling them *dead*; rather, they should be called the *undead*. They need to be watched and watched. Ask any mortuary watchman. What do you think he is put there for? Only for one thing: to keep watch, so that the dead don't crawl all over the place. There can even occur what are, in a certain sense, amusing incidents. One deceased crawled out of the mortuary while the attendant, on management's orders, was taking his bath, crawled into the disinfection room and ate up a heap of bed linen. The disinfectors dished out a damned good thrashing to the deceased in question but, as for the ruined linen, they had to settle up for that out of their own pockets. And another deceased crawled as far as the maternity ward and so frightened the inmates that one child-bearer produced a premature foetus on the spot, while the deceased pounced smartly on the fruits of the miscarriage and began to devour it, champing away vigorously. And, when a brave nurse struck the deceased on the back with a stool, he bit the said nurse on the leg and she soon died from infection by corpse poisoning. Yes, indeed, the dead are a category to be reckoned with all right, and with them you certainly have to be on the qui vive.

– Stop! – said I to my own thoughts. – You are talking nonsense. The dead are immobile.

– All right, then – my own thoughts said to me. – Just you enter your room and you'll soon find what you call an immobile dead person.

An unexpected stubbornness within me began speaking.

– All right, I will! – I replied resolutely to my own thoughts.

– Just you try! – my own thoughts said to me derisively.

This derision definitively enraged me. I grabbed the croquet mallet and rushed towards the door.

– Hold on a moment! – my own thoughts yelled at me. But I had already turned the key and unlocked the door.

The old woman was lying in the doorway, her face pressed against the floor.

Croquet mallet raised, I stood at the ready. The old woman wasn't moving.

My trembling passed off and my thoughts were flowing clearly and logically. I was in control.

– First of all, shut the door! – I commanded myself.

I pulled the key from the outer side of the door and put it into the inner side. I did this with my left hand, while in my right hand I held the croquet mallet and the whole time did not take my eyes off the old woman. I turned the key in the door and, carefully stepping over the old woman, stepped out into the middle of the room.

– Now you and I will settle things – said I. A plan had occurred to me, one to which murderers in detective stories and reports in the newspapers usually resort; I simply wanted to hide the old woman in a suitcase, carry her off out of town and dump her in a bog. I knew one such place.

I had a suitcase under the couch. I dragged it out and opened it. There were a few assorted things in it: several books, an old felt hat and some torn underwear. I unpacked all this on the couch.

At this moment the outside door slammed loudly and it seemed to me that the old woman shuddered.

I immediately jumped up and grabbed the croquet mallet.

The old woman is lying there quietly. I am standing and listening intently. It is the engine driver who has just come back; I can hear him walking about in his room. That's him going along the corridor to the kitchen. If Mar'ia Vasil'evna tells him all about my madness it will do no good. It's a devilish nuisance! I'd better go along to the kitchen and reassure them by my appearance.

I again strode over the old woman, placed the mallet right by the door, so that on my return, without even entering the room, I could have the mallet in my hands, and went out into the corridor. Voices came towards me from the kitchen, but the words were not audible. I shut the door to my room behind me and cautiously went off to the kitchen: I wanted to find out what Mar'ia Vasil'evna and the engine driver were talking about. I passed down the corridor quickly and slowed my steps near the kitchen. The engine driver was speaking; evidently he was talking about something which had happened to him at work.

I went in. The engine driver was standing with a towel in his hands and speaking, while Mar'ia Vasil'evna was sitting on a stool listening. Upon seeing me, the engine driver waved at me.

– Hello there, hello there, Matvei Filippovich – I said to him and went on through to the bathroom. So far everything was safe enough. Mar'ia Vasil'evna was used to my strange ways and may even have forgotten this latest incident.

Suddenly it dawned upon me that I had not locked the door. What if the old woman should crawl out of the room?

I rushed back but recollected myself in time and, so as not to alarm the tenants, ambled through the kitchen at a leisurely step.

Mar'ia Vasil'evna was tapping her finger on the kitchen table and saying to the engine driver:

– Quaite raight. That's quaite raight! I wud hae wustled too!

With my heart sinking, I went out into the corridor and immediately breaking very nearly into a run I dashed down to my room. The old woman, as before, was lying there quietly, her face pressed to the floor. The croquet mallet was standing by the door in the same spot. I picked it up, went into the room, and locked the door behind me with the key. Yes, there was definitely a whiff of dead body in the room. I strode over the old woman, went up to the window and sat down in the armchair. So long as I don't get ill from this so far only weak, but still already unbearable, smell. I lit up my pipe. I felt a touch of nausea and my stomach was aching a bit.

So, why am I just sitting here? I need to act quickly, before this old woman rots completely. But, in any case, I need to be careful shoving her into the suitcase because, while we're at it, she could take a nip at my hand. And, as for dying from corpse poisoning – no thank you!

– Hey, though! – I suddenly exclaimed. – I'd like to see what you would bite me with! Your teeth are over there, anyway!

I leaned over in the armchair and looked into the corner on the other side of the window where, by my reckoning, the old woman's set of dentures must be. But the false teeth were not there.

I thought for a bit: perhaps the dead old woman had been crawling about my room looking for her teeth? Perhaps she had even found them and stuck them back into her mouth?

I took the croquet mallet and poked around in the corner with it. No, the dentures had gone. Then I pulled out of the cupboard a thick flannelette sheet and went over to the old woman. The croquet mallet I held at the ready in my right hand and in my left I held the flannelette sheet.

This dead old woman was arousing a squeamish feeling of fear. I raised her head with the mallet: her mouth was open, the eyes rolled upwards and, on the whole of her chin, where I had landed my kick, a big dark bruise was spreading. I looked into the old woman's mouth. No, she had not found her dentures. I released her head. The head dropped and knocked against the floor.

Then I spread the flannelette sheet out on the floor and pulled it over to the old woman herself. Then with my foot and the croquet mallet I turned the old woman over by way of her left side on to her back. Now she was lying on the sheet. The old woman's legs were bent at the knees and her fists clasped to her shoulders. The old woman seemed to be lying on her back, like a cat, ready to defend herself from a predatory eagle. Quickly, away with this carrion!

I rolled the old woman up in the thick sheet and picked her up in my arms. She turned out to be lighter than I had thought. I put her down into the suitcase and tried to close it. I now expected all kinds of difficulties, but the lid closed comparatively easily. I clicked down the locks on the case and straightened up.

The suitcase is standing before me with a totally decorous air, as though it contains clothes and books. I took hold of it by the handle and tried to lift it. Yes, of course, it was heavy, but not excessively so. I could certainly carry it to the tram.

I looked at my watch: twenty past five. That's fine. I sat down in the armchair so as to have a breather and finish smoking my pipe.

Obviously the saveloys which I had eaten today had been a bit off, since my stomach was aching more and more. But perhaps this was because I had eaten them raw? But perhaps my stomach-ache was purely nervous.

I sit there, smoking. And minute after minute goes by.

The spring sun is shining in through the window and I screw up my eyes against its rays. Now it is hiding behind a chimney of the building opposite and the shadow of the chimney runs along the roof, flies across the street and falls right on my face. I recall how yesterday at this same time I was sitting writing my story. Here it is: the squared paper and on it the inscription, in tiny handwriting: 'The miracle worker was on the tall side'.

I looked out of the window. An invalid was walking along the street on an artificial leg, knocking loudly with his leg and with a stick. Two workmen, and an old woman with them, were holding their sides, guffawing at the invalid's ridiculous gait.

I got up. It was time! Time to be on my way! Time to take the old woman off to the bog! I still needed to borrow some money from the engine driver.

I went out into the corridor and went up to his door.

– Matvei Filippovich, are you in? – I asked.

– I'm in – replied the engine driver.

– Excuse me then, Matvei Filippovich, you don't happen to have plenty of money on you, do you? I get paid the day after tomorrow. You couldn't lend me thirty roubles, could you?

– I could – said the engine driver. And I could hear him jangling keys as he unlocked some box or other. Then he opened the door and held out a new, red thirty-rouble note.

– Thank you very much, Matvei Filippovich – I said.

– That's all right, that's all right – said the engine driver.

I stuffed the money in my pocket and returned to my room. The suitcase was calmly standing on the same spot.

– Now then, on our way, without further ado – I said to myself.

I took the suitcase and went out of the room.

Mar'ia Vasil'evna caught sight of me with the suitcase and shouted: – Where are ye off to?

– To see my aunt – said I.

– Will ye soon be back? – asked Mar'ia Vasil'evna.

– Yes – I said. – I just have to take some clothes over to my aunt. I'll be back maybe even today.

I went out on to the street. I got safely to the tram, carrying the suitcase first in my right hand, then in my left.

I got on to the tram from the front passenger space of the rear car and began waving the conductress over, so that she should come and take the money for my ticket and baggage. I didn't want to pass my single thirty-rouble note down the whole car and couldn't bring myself to leave the suitcase and myself walk through to the conductress. The conductress came over to me on to the front platform and declared that she had no change. I had to get off at the very first stop.

I stood there fuming as I was waiting for the next tram. I was suffering from stomach-ache and a slight shiver in the legs.

And then suddenly I glimpsed my delightful young lady: she was crossing the street and not looking in my direction.

I grabbed the suitcase and rushed after her. I didn't know her name and couldn't call her. The suitcase was a serious hindrance: I was holding it in front of me with both hands and pushing at it with my knees and stomach. The delightful young lady was fairly fleet of foot and I felt that I had no hope of catching her. I was soaked through with sweat and quite exhausted. The delightful young lady turned into a side-street. When I got to the corner, she was nowhere to be seen.

– That blasted old woman! – I spat, throwing the suitcase down. The sleeves of my jacket were soaked through with sweat and they stuck to my arms. I sat down on the suitcase and, pulling out my handkerchief, I wiped my neck and face with it. Two urchins stopped in front of me and began looking at me. I put on a calm face and looked attentively at the nearest gateway, as though waiting for someone. The urchins were whispering and making rude gestures towards me. A wild fury smothered me. Oh, may they be infected with tetanus!

And so, because of these obnoxious urchins, I stand up, lift the suitcase, take it over to the gateway and peer into it. I affect a surprised face, get out my watch and shrug my shoulders. The urchins are observing me from afar. I once more shrug my shoulders and peer into the gateway.

– That's strange – I say aloud; I take the suitcase and drag it to the tram stop.

I arrived at the station at five to seven. I take a return ticket to Lis'ii Nos and get on to the train.

In the carriage, apart from me, there are two others: one evidently is a workman; he is tired and is asleep, his cap pulled over his eyes. The other is quite a young fellow, dressed like a village dandy: under his jacket he is waring a pink Russian shirt and from underneath his cap protrudes a curly quiff. He is smoking a Russian cigarette, stuck into a bright green plastic cigarette holder.

I place the suitcase between the seats and sit down. I have such spasms in my stomach that I clench my fists, so as not to groan out loud with the pain.

Two militiamen are leading some citizen or other along the

platform under arrest. He is walking with his hands behind his back and his head drooping.

The train moves off. I look at my watch: ten past seven.

Oh, with what pleasure will I dump this old woman in the bog! It's a pity only that I didn't bring a stick with me, as the old woman is bound to need a few shoves.

The dandy in the pink shirt keeps looking at me impudently. I turn my back on him and look out of the window.

Horrific seizures are raging in my belly; then I have to grit my teeth, clench my fists and strain my legs.

We go through Lanskaya and Novaya Derevnya. Here there's a glitter from the golden top of the Buddhist pagoda and over there a glimpse of the sea.

But at this point I jump up and, forgetting everything around me, run off to the toilet with short steps. My consciousness is being buffeted and twisted by a reckless wave . . .

The train slackens speed. We are arriving at Lakhta. I sit there, afraid to move, lest I get thrown out of the toilet while at the station.

— If only it would hurry up and get moving! Hurry up and get moving!

The train moves off and I close my eyes in ecstasy. Oh, these minutes are just as sweet as any moments of love! All my powers are straining, but I know that this will be followed by an awful collapse.

The train is stopping again. It's Ol'gino. That means the same torture again!

But now it's a matter of phantom urges. A cold sweat comes out on my brow and a slight coldness flutters around my heart. I raise myself up and for a certain time stand with my head pressed to the wall. The train goes on and the swaying of the carriage feels quite pleasant to me.

I gather all my strength and stagger out from the toilet.

There's no one in the carriage. The worker and the dandy in the pink shirt obviously got out at Lakhta, or at Ol'gino. I walk slowly towards my window.

And suddenly I stop in my tracks and peer dully in front of me. There, where I had left it, there is no suitcase. I must have mistaken the window. I jump over to the next window. No suitcase. I jump backwards and forwards, run up and down the carriage on both sides, look under the seats, but the suitcase is nowhere to be found.

Indeed, is there any reason to doubt it? Of course, while I was in the toilet the suitcase was stolen. That could even have been predicted!

I am sitting on the seat goggle-eyed and for some reason I remember the cracking sound of the enamel coming off the overheated saucepan at Sakerdon Mikhailovich's.

– So what's the outcome? – I ask myself. – Now who will believe that I didn't kill the old woman? They'll catch me this very day, either right here or in the city at the station, like that citizen who was walking along with his head drooping.

I go out on to the outside space at the end of the carriage. The train is coming in to Lis'ii Nos. The white posts which mark off the track are flashing past. The train is stopping. The steps down from my carriage do not reach the ground. I jump down and walk over to the station office. There is still half an hour before the train back to town.

I walk over towards a little wood. There are juniper bushes there. No one will see me behind them. I make for them.

A big, green caterpillar is crawling over the ground. I drop down on my knees and touch it with my finger. Powerful and sinewy, it wriggles around a few times from one side to the other.

I look round. No one can see me. A slight shiver runs down

my back. I incline my head and quietly say:

– In the name of the Father and of the Son and of the Holy Ghost, now and for ever. Amen.

* * *

At this juncture I temporarily conclude my manuscript, considering that it is already quite long drawn out enough as it is.

(end of May and first half of June, 1939)

INCIDENTS

Dedicated to Marina Vladimirovna Malich

(1933–1937)

(1) Blue Notebook No. 10

(or 'The Red-Haired Man')

There was a red-haired man who had no eyes or ears. Neither did he have any hair, so he was called red-haired theoretically.

He couldn't speak, since he didn't have a mouth. Neither did he have a nose.

He didn't even have any arms or legs. He had no stomach and he had no back and he had no spine and he had no innards whatsoever. He had nothing at all! Therefore there's no knowing whom we are even talking about.

In fact it's better that we don't say any more about him.

(1937)

(2) Incidents

One day Orlov stuffed himself with mashed peas and died. And Krylov, on finding out about this, also died. And Spiridonov died of his own accord. And Spiridonov's wife fell off the sideboard and also died. And Spiridonov's children drowned in the pond. And Spiridonov's grandmother hit the bottle and took to the road. And Mikhailovich stopped combing his hair and went down with mange. And Kruglov sketched a woman with a whip in her hands and went out of his mind. And Perekhrestov received four hundred roubles by wire and put on such airs that he got chucked out of work.

They are good people all – but they can't keep their feet firmly on the ground.

(1933)

(3) The Plummeting Old Women

A certain old woman, out of excessive curiosity, fell out of a window, plummeted to the ground, and was smashed to pieces.

Another old woman leaned out of the window and began looking at the remains of the first one, but she also, out of excessive curiosity, fell out of the window, plummeted to the ground and was smashed to pieces.

Then a third old woman plummeted from the window, then a fourth, then a fifth.

By the time a sixth old woman had plummeted down, I was fed up watching them, and went off to Mal'tseviskiy Market where, it was said, a knitted shawl had been given to a certain blind man.

(4) A Sonnet

A surprising thing happened to me: I suddenly forgot which comes first – 7 or 8.

I went off to the neighbours and asked them what they thought on the subject.

Just imagine their and my surprise when they suddenly discovered that they too couldn't recall how to count: 1, 2, 3, 4, 5 and 6 they remembered, but they'd forgotten what followed.

We all went to the overpriced food shop, the Gastronom on the corner of Znamenskaya and Basseynaya street, and put our quandary to the cashier. The cashier smiled sadly, pulled a little hammer out of her mouth and, twitching her nose a bit, said – I should think seven comes after eight whenever eight comes after seven.

We thanked the cashier and joyfully ran out of the shop. But then, having thought about the cashier's words, we got depressed again, since her words seemed to us to be devoid of any sense.

What were we to do? We went to the Summer Garden and started counting the trees there. But, getting as far as 6, we stopped and began to argue: in the opinion of some, 7 came next, and in the opinion of others – 8.

We would have argued for ages, but fortunately then some child fell off a park bench and broke both jaw-bones. This distracted us from our argument.

And then we dispersed homewards.

(1935)

(5) Petrov and Kamarov

Petrov: Hey, Kamarov, old chap!
            Let's catch a few of these gnats!
Kamarov: No, I'm not yet up to that;
            We'd do better to catch some tom-cats!

(6) The Optical Illusion

Semyon Semyonovich, with his glasses on, looks at a pine tree and he sees: in the pine tree sits a peasant showing him his fist.

Semyon Semyonovich, with his glasses off, looks at the pine tree and sees that there is no one sitting in the pine tree.

Semyon Semyonovich, with his glasses on, looks at the pine tree and again sees that in the pine tree sits a peasant showing him his fist.

Semyon Semyonovich, with his glasses off, again sees that there is no one sitting in the pine tree.

Semyon Semyonovich, with his glasses on again, looks at the pine tree and again sees that in the pine tree sits a peasant showing him his fist.

Semyon Semyonovich doesn't wish to believe in this phenomenon and considers this phenomenon an optical illusion.

(1934)

(7) Pushkin and Gogol

GOGOL *falls out from the wings on to the stage and quietly lies there.*
PUSHKIN *appears on stage, stumbles over* GOGOL *and falls.*

PUSHKIN What the devil! Seems I've tripped over Gogol!

GOGOL (*Getting up*) What a vile abomination! You can't even have a rest. (*Walks off, stumbles over* PUSHKIN *and falls*) Seems I've stumbled over Pushkin!

PUSHKIN (*Getting up*) Not a minute's peace! (*Walks off, stumbles over* GOGOL *and falls*) What the devil! Seems I've tripped over Gogol again!

GOGOL (*Getting up*) Always an obstacle in everything! (*Walks off, stumbles over* PUSHKIN *and falls*) It's a vile abomination! Tripped over Pushkin again!

PUSHKIN (*Getting up*) Hooliganism! Sheer hooliganism! (*Walks off, stumbles over* GOGOL *and falls*) What the devil! Tripped over Gogol again!

GOGOL (*Getting up*) It's sheer mockery! (*Walks off, stumbles over* PUSHKIN *and falls*) Tripped over Pushkin again!

PUSHKIN (*Getting up*) What the devil! Well, really, what the devil! (*Walks off, stumbles over* GOGOL *and falls*) Over Gogol!

GOGOL (*Getting up*) Vile abomination! (*Walks off, stumbles over* PUSHKIN *and falls*) Over Pushkin!

PUSHKIN (*Getting up*) What the devil! (*Walks off, stumbles over* GOGOL *and falls into the wings*) Over Gogol!

GOGOL (*Getting up*) Vile abomination! (*Walks off into wings; from offstage*) Over Pushkin!

(*Curtain*) (*1934*)

(8) The Carpenter Kushakov

Once there was a carpenter. He was called Kushakov.

One day he left his house and went off to the shop to buy some carpenter's glue.

There had been a thaw and it was very slippery on the street.

The carpenter took a few steps, slipped, fell down and cracked his forehead open.

– Ugh! – said the carpenter, got up, went off to the chemist's, bought a plaster and stuck it on his forehead.

But when he went out on to the street he again slipped, fell and smashed his nose.

– Huh! – said the carpenter, went off to the chemist's, bought a plaster and stuck the plaster over his nose.

Then he went out on to the street again, again slipped, fell and cracked open his cheek.

Once again he had to go off to the chemist's and stick a plaster over his cheek.

– Well, then – the chemist said to the carpenter – you seem to fall and hurt yourself so often, that I would advise you to buy several plasters while you are at it.

– No – said the carpenter – I'm not going to fall any more!

But when he went out on to the street he slipped again, fell and smashed his chin.

– Poxy icy patches! – exclaimed the carpenter and again ran off to the chemist's.

– There you are, you see – said the chemist. – You've gone and fallen again.

– Not at all! – shouted the carpenter. – I won't hear another word! Give me a plaster, and hurry up!

The chemist handed over a plaster; the carpenter stuck it on his chin and ran off home.

But at home they didn't recognize him and wouldn't let him in to the flat.

– I'm the carpenter Kushakov! – the carpenter shouted.

– Pull the other one! – was the reply from the flat and they fastened the door, both with the key and with the chain.

The carpenter Kushakov stood on the staircase for a bit, spat and went off down the street.

(9) The Trunk

A thin-necked man climbed into a trunk, shut the lid behind him and began gasping for breath.

– So – said the thin-necked man, gasping for breath – I am gasping for breath in this trunk because I've got a thin neck. The lid of the trunk is down and isn't letting any air in. I shall be gasping for breath, but all the same I won't open the lid of the trunk. I shall be gradually dying. I shall see the struggle of life and death. The battle which takes place will be an unnatural one, with the chances equal, because under natural conditions death triumphs, and life, doomed to death, merely struggles in vain with the enemy, clinging until the last minute to a futile hope. But in the struggle which will take place now, life will be cognizant of the means of victory: to achieve this life will have to force my hands to open the lid of the trunk. We shall see who will win! Only there's an awful smell of naphthalene. If life triumphs I shall powder all the things in the trunk with makhorka.* So, it has begun: I can't breathe any more. I'm finished, that's clear. There's no saving me now! And there are no lofty thoughts in my head. I'm suffocating!

– Hey! What's that then? Something just happened but I can't make out exactly what. I saw something or heard something ...

– Hey! Something happened again. My God! There's nothing to breath. It seems I'm dying ...

– And now what's that then? Why am I singing? My neck seems to be hurting ... But where's the trunk? Why can I see all the things in the room? And I seem to be lying on the floor! But where's the trunk?

The man with the thin neck got up from the floor and looked round. The trunk was nowhere around. On the chairs and on the bed lay things which had been pulled out of the trunk, but the trunk was nowhere around.

The thin-necked man said: – So, life has triumphed over death by means unknown to me.

* cheap, coarse tobacco.

(10) The Incident with Petrakov

And so on one occasion Petrakov wanted to lie down for a sleep but, lying down, he missed the bed. He hit the floor so hard that he just lies on the floor and can't get up.

And so Petrakov made a supreme effort and got up on all fours. But his strength deserted him and he again fell down on his stomach and just lies there.

Petrakov lay on the floor for five hours. At first he just lay there and then he fell asleep.

Sleep restored Petrakov's energy. He awoke completely refreshed, got up, walked up and down the room and lay down cautiously on the bed. 'Well – he thought – now I'll have a sleep.' But he just didn't feel sleepy. Petrakov turns over on to one side and then the other, but cannot get to sleep at all.

And that's just about it.

(11) The Story of the Fighting Men

Aleksey Alekseyevich held Andrey Karlovich down in a crushing lock and, having smashed him in the mug, let him go.

Andrey Karlovich, pale with fury, flung himself at Aleksey Alekseyevich and banged him in the teeth.

Aleksey Alekseyevich, not expecting such a swift onslaught, collapsed on the floor, whereupon Andrey Karlovich sat astride him, pulled his set of dentures from his mouth and gave Aleksey Alekseyevich such a going over with them that Aleksey Alekseyevich rose from the floor with his face completely mutilated and his nostril ripped open. Holding his face in his hands, Aleksey Alekseyevich ran off.

Whereas Andrey Karlovich gave his dentures a rub,

inserted them in his mouth with a click of the teeth and, having satisfied himself as to the placement of his dentures, he took stock of his surroundings and, not seeing Aleksey Alekseyevich, set off in search of him.

(1936)

(12) The Dream

Kalugin fell asleep and had a dream that he was sitting in some bushes and a policeman was walking past the bushes.

Kalugin woke up, scratched his mouth and went to sleep again and had another dream that he was walking past some bushes and that a policeman had hidden in the bushes and was sitting there.

Kalugin woke up, put a newspaper under his head, so as not to wet the pillow with his dribblings, and went to sleep again; and again he had a dream that he was sitting in some bushes and a policeman was walking past the bushes.

Kalugin woke up, changed the newspaper, lay down and went to sleep again. He fell asleep and had another dream that he was walking past some bushes and a policeman was sitting in the bushes.

At this point Kalugin woke up and decided not to sleep any more, but he immediately fell asleep and had a dream that he was sitting behind a policeman and some bushes were walking past.

Kalugin let out a yell and tossed about in bed but couldn't wake up.

Kalugin slept straight through for four days and four nights and on the fifth day he awoke so emaciated that he had to tie his boots to his feet with string, so that they didn't fall off. In the bakery where Kalugin always bought wheaten bread, they didn't recognize him and handed him a half-rye loaf.

And a sanitary commission which was going round the apartments, on catching sight of Kalugin, decided that he was insanitary and no use for anything and instructed the janitors to throw Kalugin out with the rubbish.

Kalugin was folded in two and thrown out as rubbish.

(13) The Mathematician and
Andrey Semyonovich

MATHEMATICIAN	(*Pulling a ball out of his head*)
	I've pulled a ball out of my head.
	I've pulled a ball out of my head.
	I've pulled a ball out of my head.
	I've pulled a ball out of my head.
ANDREY SEMYONOVICH	Put it back.
	Put it back.
	Put it back.
	Put it back.
MATHEMATICIAN	No, I won't!
	No, I won't!
	No, I won't!
	No, I won't!

ANDREY SEMYONOVICH	Well, don't then.
	Well, don't then.
	Well, don't then.
MATHEMATICIAN	So I won't, then!
	So I won't, then!
	So I won't, then!
ANDREY SEMYONOVICH	Well, that's okay.
	Well, that's okay.
	Well, that's okay.
MATHEMATICIAN	So, I won!
	So, I won!
	So, I won!
ANDREY SEMYONOVICH	All right, you won, so now calm down!
MATHEMATICIAN	No, I won't calm down!
	No, I won't calm down!
	No, I won't calm down!
ANDREY SEMYONOVICH	You may be a mathematician but, my word, you're not very bright.
MATHEMATICIAN	No, I'm bright and I know an awful lot!
	No, I'm bright and I know an awful lot!
	No, I'm bright and I know an awful lot!
ANDREY SEMYONOVICH	A lot, yes, only it's all rubbish.
MATHEMATICIAN	No, it's not rubbish!
	No, it's not rubbish!
	No, it's not rubbish!
ANDREY SEMYONOVICH	I'm fed up with arguing with you!
MATHEMATICIAN	No, I'm not fed up!
	No, I'm not fed up!
	No, I'm not fed up!

ANDREY SEMYONOVICH *waves his hand in annoyance and walks away*. THE MATHEMATICIAN *after standing for a minute, walks off after* ANDREY SEMYONOVICH.

(Curtain)

(1933)

(14) The Young Man who Astonished a Watchman

– As for you! – said the watchman, examining a fly. – If I smeared it with carpenter's glue, then that would very likely be the end of it. What a laugh! Just with a bit of glue!

– Hey you, leprechaun! – a young man in yellow gloves hailed the watchman.

The watchman immediately realized that this was addressed to him, but he continued looking at the fly.

– I'm talking to you, aren't I? – the young man shouted again. – You yahoo!

The watchman crushed the fly with his finger and, without turning his head to the young man, said:

– Who do you think you're bawling at, you cheeky bugger? I can hear you all right. There's no need to bawl like that!

The young man brushed his trousers down with his gloves and asked, in a refined voice: – Tell me, old chap, how do I get to heaven from here?

The watchman stared at the young man, screwed up one eye, then screwed up the other, then scratched his beard, stared at the young man again and said: — There's nothing to hang about here for, go on, on your way.

— Excuse me — said the young man — it's an urgent matter for me. There's even a room ready booked for me there.

— Okay — said the watchman — show me your ticket.

— I haven't got a ticket on me; they said I'd be let in, just like that — said the young man, looking the watchman in the eye.

— As for you! — said the watchman.

— So, what about it, then? — said the young man. — Are you going to let me through?

— Okay, okay — said the watchman. — Go on, then.

— And how do I get there? Where is it? — asked the young man. — You see, I don't know the way.

— Where do you need to go? — asked the watchman, putting on a severe look.

The young man covered his face with the palm of his hand and said very quietly: — To heaven!

The watchman leaned forward, moved his right leg so as to stand up more firmly, looked at the young man intently and asked sternly:

— What are you doing? Playing the bloody fool?

The young man smiled, raised his hand in its yellow glove, waved it above his head and suddenly disappeared.

The watchman sniffed the air. There was a smell in the air of burnt feathers.

— As for you! — said the watchman; he unzipped his jerkin, scratched his stomach, spat on the spot where the young man had stood and slowly went off to his hut.

(1936)

(15) Four Illustrations of How a New Idea Disconcerts a Man Unprepared for It

1.

WRITER   I'm a writer.

READER   In my opinion you're shit!

THE WRITER *stands for a few minutes, shaken by this new idea, and falls down in a dead faint. He is carried out.*

2.

ARTIST   I'm an artist.

WORKER   In my opinion you're shit!

THE ARTIST *turns as white as a sheet, sways like a thin reed and unexpectedly expires. He is carried out.*

3.

COMPOSER   I'm a Composer.

VANYA RUBLYOV   In my opinion you're ...!

THE COMPOSER, *breathing heavily, sank back. He is unexpectedly carried out.*

4.

CHEMIST   I'm a chemist.

PHYSICIST   In my opinion you're ...!

THE CHEMIST *said not another word and collapsed heavily to the floor.*

(16) Losses

Andrey Andreyevich Myasov bought a wick at the market and carried it off homewards.

On the way, Andrey Andreyevich lost the wick and went into a shop to buy 150 grams of Poltava sausage. Then Andrey Andreyevich went into the dairy and bought a bottle of curds, then he drank a small mug of kvass at a stall and joined the queue for a newspaper. The queue was a rather long one and Andrey Andreyevich stood for no less than twenty minutes in the queue, and when he reached the newspaper seller the newspaper ran out right in front of his nose.

Andrey Andreyevich was stymied and he went off home, but on the way he lost the curds and dropped into the bakery, where he bought a stick of French bread, but lost the Poltava sausage.

Then Andrey Andreyevich went straight home, but on the way he fell down, lost the French bread and broke his pince-nez.

Andrey Andreyevich reached home in a very bad mood and straight away went to bed, but could not get to sleep for a long time and when he did get to sleep he had a dream: he dreamt that he had lost his toothbrush and that he was cleaning his teeth with some sort of a candlestick.

(17) Makarov and Petersen

(subtitled 'No. 3')

MAKAROV	Here, in this book, is written all concerning our desires and their fulfilment. Read this book, and you will understand how empty are our desires. You will also understand how easy it is to fulfil another's desire and how difficult to fulfil one's own desire.
PETERSEN	You didn't half say that solemnly. That's how Indian chiefs speak.
MAKAROV	This is such a book that it must be spoken of in elevated tones. When I so much as think of it I take off my hat.
PETERSEN	Do you wash your hands before you touch it, then?
MAKAROV	Yes, and the hands must be washed.
PETERSEN	You ought to wash your feet, to be on the safe side.
MAKAROV	That was most unwitty and rude.
PETERSEN	But what is this book?
MAKAROV	The name of this book is secret ...
PETERSEN	Tee-hee-hee!
MAKAROV	This book is called *Malgil*.

PETERSEN *disappears*.

MAKAROV	Good Lord! What's this, then? Petersen!
VOICE OF PETERSEN	What's happened? Makarov! Where am I?

MAKAROV	Where are you? I can't see you.
VOICE OF PETERSEN	And where are you? I can't see you either. What are these spheres?
MAKAROV	What can we do? Petersen, can you hear me?
VOICE OF PETERSEN	I can hear you! But whatever's happened? And what are these spheres?
MAKAROV	Can you move?
VOICE OF PETERSEN	Makarov! Can you see these spheres?
MAKAROV	What spheres?
VOICE OF PETERSEN	Let me go! ... Let me go! ... Makarov!

Silence. MAKAROV *stands in horror, then grabs the book and opens it.*

MAKAROV	(*Reads*) ... 'Gradually man loses his form and becomes a sphere. And, once a sphere, man loses all his desires.'

(Curtain)

(1934)

(18) Lynch Law

Petrov gets on his horse and, addressing the crowd, makes a speech about what will happen if, in the place where the public park now is, an American skyscraper will be built. The crowd listens and evidently is in agreement. Petrov notes down something for himself in his notebook. From the crowd there may be distinguished a man of average height who asks Petrov what he has written down for himself in his notebook. Petrov replies that this concerns only himself. The man of average height persists. One word leads to another: and strife ensues. The crowd takes the side of the man of average height and Petrov, preserving his skin, urges on his horse and makes off round the bend. The crowd gets agitated and, for the lack of another victim, grabs the man of average height and tears off his head. The torn off head rolls down the pavement and gets stuck in an open drain. The crowd, having satisfied its passions, disperses.

(19) An Encounter

On one occasion a man went off to work and on the way he met another man who, having bought a loaf of Polish bread, was wending his way home.

And that's just about all there is to it.

(20) An Unsuccessful Show

On to the stage comes PETRAKOV-GORBUNOV, *who wants to say something but hiccups. He starts to throw up. He leaves.*

Enter PRITYKIN.

PRITYKIN   Our esteemed Petrakov-Gorbunov has to ann
             ... (*He throws up and runs off stage.*)

Enter MAKAROV.

MAKAROV   Yegor ... (*Makarov throws up. He runs off.*)

Enter SERPUKHOV.

SERPUKHOV   So as not to be ... (*He throws up and runs off.*)

Enter KUROVA.

KUROVA   I would have ... (*She throws up and runs off.*)

Enter a LITTLE GIRL.

LITTLE GIRL Daddy asked me to let you all know that the
             theatre is closing. We are all being sick!

(*Curtain*)

(21) Clunk

*Summer. A writing table. A door to the right. A picture on the wall.
The picture is a drawing of a horse, the horse has a gypsy in its teeth.*
OLGA PETROVNA *is chopping wood. At every blow Olga Petrovna's
pince-nez leaps from her nose.* YEVDOKIM OSIPOVICH *is seated in an
armchair smoking.*

OLGA PETROVNA	(*Strikes with the chopper at the log, which, however, does not as much as splinter*)
YEVDOKIM OSIPOVICH	Clunk!
OLGA PETROVNA	(*Putting on her pince-nez, swipes at the log*)
YEVDOKIM OSIPOVICH	Clunk!
OLGA PETROVNA	(*Putting on her pince-nez, swipes at the log*)
YEVDOKIM OSIPOVICH	Clunk!
OLGA PETROVNA	(*Putting on her pince-nez, swipes at the log*)
YEVDOKIM OSIPOVICH	Clunk!
OLGA PETROVNA	(*Putting on her pince-nez*) Yevdokim Osipovich! I implore you, don't keep saying that word 'clunk'.
YEVDOKIM OSIPOVICH	Very well, very well.
OLGA PETROVNA	(*Striking with the chopper at the log*)
YEVDOKIM OSIPOVICH	Clunk!
OLGA PETROVNA	Yevdokim Osipovich. You promised not to keep saying that word 'clunk'.
YEVDOKIM OSIPOVICH	Very well, very well, Olga Petrovna. I won't any more.
OLGA PETROVNA	(*Striking with the chopper at log*)
YEVDOKIM OSIPOVICH	Clunk!
OLGA PETROVNA	(*Putting on her pince-nez*) This is

disgraceful. A grown-up, middle-aged man, and he doesn't understand a simple human request.

YEVDOKIM OSIPOVICH Olga Petrovna! You may carry on with your work in peace. I won't disturb you any more.

OLGA PETROVNA I implore you, I really implore you: let me chop this log at least.

YEVDOKIM OSIPOVICH Chop away, of course you can, chop away.

OLGA PETROVNA (*Striking with chopper at log*)

YEVDOKIM OSIPOVICH Clunk!

OLGA PETROVNA *drops the chopper, opens her mouth, but is unable to say anything.* YEVDOKIM OSIPOVICH *gets up from the armchair, looks* OLGA PETROVNA *up and down and slowly walks away.* OLGA PETROVNA *stands immobile, mouth open, and gazes after the retreating* YEVDOKIM OSIPOVICH.

(*Slow curtain*)

(22) What They Sell in the Shops These Days

Koratygin came to see Tikakeyev but didn't find him in.

At that time Tikakeyev was at the shop buying sugar, meat and cucumbers.

Koratygin hung about by Tikakeyev's door and was just thinking of scribbling a note when he suddenly looked up to see Tikakeyev himself coming, carrying in his arms an oilskin bag.

Koratygin spotted Tikakeyev and shouted: – I've been waiting a whole hour for you!

– That's not true – said Tikakeyev – I've only been out of the house twenty-five minutes.

– Well, I don't know about that – said Koratygin – except that I've already been here a whole hour.

– Don't tell lies – said Tikakeyev – you should be ashamed to lie.

– My dear fellow! – said Koratygin – Be so good as to be a little more particular with your expressions.

– I consider . . . – began Tikakeyev, but Koratygin interrupted him:

– If you consider . . . – he said, but at this point Tikakeyev interrupted Koratygin and said:

– A fine one you are!

These words put Koratygin into such a frenzy that he pressed a finger against one of his nostrils and through his other nostril blew snot at Tikakeyev.

Then Tikakeyev pulled the biggest cucumber out of his bag and hit Koratygin across the head with it.

Koratygin clutched at his head with his hands, fell down and died.

That's the size of the cucumbers sold in the shops these days!

(23) Mashkin Killed Koshkin

Comrade Koshkin danced around Comrade Mashkin.

Comrade Mashkin followed Comrade Koshkin with his eyes.

Comrade Koshkin insultingly waved his arms and repulsively shook his legs.

Comrade Mashkin put on a frown.

Comrade Koshkin twitched his belly and stamped his right foot.

Comrade Mashkin let out a cry and flung himself at Comrade Koshkin.

Comrade Koshkin tried to run away, but stumbled and was overtaken by Comrade Mashkin.

Comrade Mashkin struck Comrade Koshkin on the head with his fist.

Comrade Koshkin let out a cry and fell to his hands and knees.

Comrade Mashkin put the boot in to Comrade Koshkin under the belly and once more struck him across the skull with his fist.

Comrade Koshkin measured his length on the floor and died.

Mashkin killed Koshkin.

(24) Sleep Teases a Man

Markov took off his boots and, with a deep breath, lay down on the divan.

He felt sleepy but, as soon as he closed his eyes, the desire for sleep immediately passed. Markov opened his eyes and stretched out his hand for a book. But sleep again came over him and, not even reaching the book, Markov lay down and once more closed his eyes. But, the moment his eyes closed, sleepiness left him again and his consciousness became so clear that Markov could solve in his head algebraical problems involving equations with two unknown quantities.

Markov was tormented for quite some time, not knowing what to do: should he sleep or should he liven himself up? Finally, exhausted and thoroughly sick of himself and his room, Markov put on his coat and hat, took his walking cane and went out on to the street. The fresh breeze calmed Makarov down, he became rather more at one with himself and felt like going back home to his room.

Upon going into his room, he experienced an agreeable bodily fatigue and felt like sleeping. But, as soon as he lay down on the divan and closed his eyes, his sleepiness instantly evaporated.

In a fury, Markov jumped up from his divan and, hatless and coatless, raced off in the direction of Tavricheskiy Park.

(25) The Hunters

Six men went hunting, but only four returned.

Two, in fact, hadn't returned.

Oknov, Kozlov, Stryuchkov and Motylkov returned home safely, but Shirokov and Kablukov perished on the hunt.

Oknov went around very upset the whole day and wouldn't even talk to anyone. Kozlov walked round behind Oknov with great persistence, badgering him with all manner of questions, by which means he drove Oknov to a point of extreme irritation.

KOZLOV	Do you fancy a smoke?
OKNOV	No!
KOZLOV	Do you want me to bring you that thing over there?
OKNOV	No!
KOZLOV	Perhaps you'd like me to tell you a funny story?
OKNOV	No!
KOZLOV	Well, do you want a drink? I've got some tea and cognac here.
OKNOV	Not content with just having smashed you over the skull with this stone, I'll rip your leg off as well.
STRYUCHKOV AND MOTYLKOV	What are you doing? What are you doing?
KOZLOV	Pick me up from the ground.
MOTYLKOV	Don't you get excited now, that wound will heal.

KOZLOV	And where's Oknov?
OKNOV	(*Ripping away at Kozlov's leg*) I'm right here.
KOZLOV	Oh, my gosh! he-elp!
STRYUCHKOV AND MOTYLKOV	Seems he's ripped the leg off him!
OKNOV	Ripped it off and thrown it over there!
STRYUCHKOV	That's atrocious!
OKNOV	Wha-at?
STRYUCHKOV	. . ocious . . .
OKNOV	What's that?
STRYUCHKOV	N-n . . . nothing.
KOZLOV	How am I going to get home?
MOTYLKOV	Don't worry, we'll fix a wooden leg on you!
STRYUCHKOV	What are you like at standing on one leg?
KOZLOV	I can do it, but I'm no great shakes at it.
STRYUCHKOV	That's all right, we'll support you.
OKNOV	Let me get at him.
STRYUCHKOV	Hey, no. You'd better go away!
OKNOV	No, let me through! . . . Let me! . . . Let . . . That's what I wanted to do.
STRYUCHKOV AND MOTYLKOV	How horrible!
OKNOV	Ha, ha, ha.
MOTYLKOV	But where is Kozlov?
STRYUCHKOV	He's crawled off into the bushes!
MOTYLKOV	Kozlov, are you there?
KOZLOV	Glug-glug!
MOTYLKOV	Now look what's become of him!
STRYUCHKOV	What's to be done with him?
MOTYLKOV	Well, we can't do a thing with him, now. In my view, we'd better just strangle him. Kozlov! Hey Kozlov! Can you hear me?
KOZLOV	O-oh, yes, but only just.

MOTYLKOV	Don't you upset yourself mate, we're just going to strangle you. Wait a minute, now! . . . There, there, there we are.
STRYUCHKOV	Here we are, and again! That's the way, yes! Come on, a bit more . . . Now, that's that!
MOTYLKOV	That's that, then!
OKNOV	Lord have mercy on him!

(26) An Historical Episode

for V.N. Petrov

Ivan Ivanovich Susanin (that same historical personage who laid down his life for the tsar and was subsequently extolled by Glinka's opera) once went into a Russian hostelry and, having sat down at a table, ordered himself an entrecôte. While the hostelry host grilled the entrecôte, Ivan Ivanovich snatched at his beard with his teeth and fell to thinking, as was his wont.

Thirty-five notches of time elapsed and mine host brought Ivan Ivanovich his entrecôte on a round wooden platter. Ivan Ivanovich was hungry and, as was the custom of the time, grabbed the entrecôte with his hands and began to eat it. But, in his haste to satisfy his hunger, Ivan Ivanovich fell upon the entrecôte so greedily that he forgot to pull his beard out of his mouth and consumed along with the entrecôte a clump of his own beard.

And thereby arose great unpleasantness, as not fifteen notches of time had elapsed when a powerful gripe attacked

Ivan Ivanovich's stomach. Ivan Ivanovich leaped up from the table and charged into the yard. Mine host began shouting to Ivan Ivanovich: – Lo, what a tufty beard you have. – But Ivan Ivanovich, paying no attention to anything, ran on into the yard.

Then the boyar Kovshegub, sitting in a corner of the hostelry drinking malt liquor, banged his fist on the table and yelled: – Who be he?

And mine host, bowing low, answered the boyar: – He be our patriot Ivan Ivanovich Susanin.

– You don't say – said the boyar, drinking up his malt liquor.

– Care for a bit of fish? – asked mine host.

– Frig off! – shouted the boyar and loosed a ladle at mine host. The ladle whistled past the head of mine host, flew out the window to the yard and smashed Ivan Ivanovich, sitting there in eagle-like pose, right in the teeth. Ivan Ivanovich clutched at his cheek with one hand and rolled on his side.

At this point Karp ran out of the stables on the right and, jumping over a trough in which, amid the slops, lay a pig, with a yell ran off towards the gates. Mine host looked out from the hostelry. – What are you bawling for? – he asked Karp. But Karp, not answering at all, ran away.

Mine host went out to the yard and spotted Susanin lying motionless on the ground. Mine host approached closer and looked him in the face. Susanin stared back at mine host.

– So, be you in one piece? – asked mine host.

– One piece, yea, but I'm worried what might clobber me next – said Susanin.

– No – said mine host – don't worry. It were the boyar Kovshegub who half killed you, but he's gorn now.

– Well, thankee God for that! – said Ivan Susanin, getting up off the ground. – A valiant man I may be, but I don't care to risk my guts for nowt. So I hugged the ground and waited: what next? First sign, and I'd have crawled right off on my guts all the way to Yeldyrin Dwellings ... Ee-eck, what a swollen cheek. Oh my Gawd! Half me beard's torn off!

— Oh, ye were like that before — said mine host.

— What d'yer mean it were like it before? — screamed the patriot Susanin. — What, you reckon I go around so, with a tufty beard?

— Aye, so — said mine host.

— Oh, a pox on you — muttered Ivan Susanin.

Mine host narrowed his eyes and, arms aflail, he sailed into Susanin and took a swing across his ear. The patriot Susanin collapsed and did not move an inch. — Take that! Pox yourself! — said mine host and retired within his hostelry.

For a few notches of time Susanin lay on the ground just listening but, hearing nothing suspicious, he cautiously raised his head and took stock. There was no one in the yard, unless we count the pig, which, having scrambled out of the trough, was now rolling in a filthy puddle. Ivan Susanin, with occasional backward glances, stealthily approached the gates. Luckily the gates were open and the patriot Ivan Susanin, writhing wormlike over the ground, crawled off in the direction of Yeldyrin Dwellings.

Here then is an episode from the life of the celebrated personage who laid down his life for the tsar and was subsequently extolled in Glinka's opera.

(1939)

(27) Fedya Davidovich

Fedya kept prowling round the butter-dish and finally, seizing the moment when his wife was bending over to cut a toe-nail, he quickly, in a single movement, took all the butter out of the butter-dish with his finger and shoved it into his mouth. As he was covering the butter-dish, Fedya accidentally clattered the lid: his wife straightened up immediately and, spotting the empty butter-dish, pointed at it with the scissors, saying in a severe tone: – The butter's not in the butter-dish. Where is it?

Fedya's eyes flashed in surprise and, extending his neck, he had a look into the butter-dish.

– That's butter you've got in your mouth – said his wife, pointing the scissors at Fedya.

Fedya began shaking his head in denial.

– Aha – said his wife – you say nothing and shake your head because your mouth's full of butter.

Fedya's eyes widened in astonishment and he waved his hands dismissively at his wife, as if to say – What do you mean? It's nothing of the kind.

But his wife said: – You're lying. Open your mouth.

– Mm, mm – said Fedya.

– Open your mouth – his wife repeated.

Fedya spread his fingers and mumbled something, as if to say – Ah yes, I almost forgot, I'll be back in a sec . . . – and stood up, intending to leave the room.

– Stay where you are! – snapped his wife.

But Fedya quickened his step and slipped out of the door. His wife darted after him but, since she was naked, she stopped by the door as in that condition she could not go out into the corridor, where other tenants of the apartment would be walking up and down.

– He's got away – said his wife, sitting down on the divan. – What a devil!

And Fedya, reaching a door along the corridor on which hung the sign 'Entry Categorically Forbidden', opened that door and went into the room.

The room which Fedya entered was narrow and long, its window curtained with newspaper. On the right-hand side of the room by the wall was a dirty, broken-down couch, and by the window a table made of planks placed at one end on a bedside table and at the other on the back of a chair. On the left-hand wall was a double shelf on which lay it was not clear what.

There was nothing else in the room, unless you count the man reclining on the couch, with a pale green face, dressed in a long and torn brown frock-coat and black nankeen trousers, from which there protruded freshly washed feet. The man was not asleep and he fixed intently on the intruder.

Fedya bowed, clicked his heels and, having pulled the butter out of his mouth, showed it to the reclining man.

– One and a half – said the host without changing his pose.

– That's not very much – said Fedya.

– It's quite enough – said the tenant of the room.

– Well, all right – said Fedya and, having removed the butter from his finger, placed it on the shelf.

– You can come for the money tomorrow morning – said the host.

– What do you mean! – exclaimed Fedya – I need it right now. And anyway only one and a half roubles is . . .

– Bugger off – said the host drily and Fedya fled the room on tiptoe, closing the door carefully behind him.

(1939)

(28) Anecdotes from the Life of Pushkin

1. Pushkin was a poet and was always writing something. Once Zhukovsky caught him at his writing and exclaimed loudly: – You're not half a scribbler!

From then on Pushkin was very fond of Zhukovsky and started to call him simply Zhukov out of friendship.

2. As we know, Pushkin's beard never grew. Pushkin was very distressed about this and he always envied Zakharin who, on the contrary, grew a perfectly respectable beard. 'His grows, but mine doesn't' – Pushkin would often say, pointing at Zakharin with his fingernails. And every time he was right.

3. Once Petrushevsky broke his watch and sent for Pushkin. Pushkin arrived, had a look at Petrushevsky's watch and put it back on the chair. 'What do you say then, Pushkin old mate?' – asked Petrushevsky. 'It's a stop-watch' – said Pushkin.

4. When Pushkin broke his legs, he started to go about on wheels. His friends used to enjoy teasing Pushkin and grabbing him by his wheels. Pushkin took this very badly and wrote abusive verses about his friends. He called these verses 'erpigrams'.

5. The summer of 1829 Pushkin spent in the country. He used to get up early in the morning, drink a jug of fresh milk and run to the river to bathe. Having bathed in the river, Pushkin would lie down on the grass and sleep until dinner. After dinner Pushkin would sleep in a hammock. If he met

any stinking peasants, Pushkin would nod at them and squeeze his nose with his fingers. And the stinking peasants would scratch their caps and say: 'It don't matter'.

6. Pushkin liked to throw stones. If he saw stones, then he would start throwing them. Sometimes he would fly into such a temper that he would stand there, red in the face, waving his arms and throwing stones. It really was rather awful!

7. Pushkin had four sons and they were all idiots. One of them couldn't even sit on his chair and kept falling off. Pushkin himself was not very good at sitting on his chair, either. It used to be quite hilarious: they would be sitting at the table; at one end Pushkin would keep falling off his chair, and at the other end – his son. What a pain these saints can be!

(29) The Start of a
Very Nice Summer's Day

A Symphony

No sooner had the cock crowed than Timofey jumped out of his window on to the roof and frightened everyone who was passing down the street at that time. Khariton the peasant stopped, picked up a stone and shied it at Timofey. Timofey disappeared somewhere.

– What a dodger! – cried the human herd and a certain Zubov took a run and nonchalantly accelerated head-first into the wall.

– Oo-er! – exclaimed a peasant woman with a swollen cheek. But Komarov gave this woman a swift left-right and the woman ran off howling into a gateway. Feteliushin walked past and laughed. Komarov went up to him and said:

– As for you, you fat lump! – and struck Feteliushin in the stomach. Feteliushin supported himself against the wall and started to hiccup. Romashkin spat out of his window from above, trying to hit Feteliushin. At this point, not far away, a big-nosed woman was hitting her child with a trough. And a young, rather hefty mother was rubbing her pretty little girl's face against a brick wall. A small dog, which had broken its thin leg, was sprawled on the pavement. A small boy was eating something revolting from a spittoon. There was a long queue for sugar at the grocery shop. Women were swearing loudly and shoving each other with their bags. Khariton the peasant, having just downed some methylated spirit, was standing in front of the women with his trousers undone and uttering bad language.

This was the way that a nice summer's day would start.

(30) Pakin and Rakukin

You, cut out that snottering! – said Pakin to Rakukin.

Rakukin wrinkled up his nose and looked most uncordially at Pakin.

– What are you looking at? Seen enough yet? – asked Pakin.

Rakukin chewed at his lips and, indignant in his revolving armchair, began looking the other way. Pakin drummed on his knee with his fingers and said:

– What a fool! I'd like to take a good stick to his skull.

Rakukin stood up and started to walk out of the room, but Pakin quickly leapt up, caught up with Rakukin and said:

– Wait a minute! Where d'ye think you're rushing off to? Better sit down, I've something to show you.

Rakukin stopped and looked distrustfully at Pakin.

– What, don't you believe me? – asked Pakin.

– I believe you – said Rakukin.

– Well then, sit down here, in this armchair – said Pakin.

And Rakukin sat down again in his revolving armchair.

– So, then – said Pakin – what are you sitting in that chair for, like a fool?

Rakukin moved his legs about and began a rapid blinking of the eyes.

– Don't blink – said Pakin.

Rakukin stopped blinking and, adopting a hunched posture, drew his head in to his shoulders.

– Sit straight – said Pakin.

Rakukin, continuing to sit hunched up, stuck out his belly and extended his neck.

– Ee – said Pakin – I couldn't half give you a smack in the kisser!

Rakukin hiccupped, puffed out his cheeks, and then carefully emitted the air through his nostrils.

– Now, you, stop that snottering! – said Pakin to Rakukin.

Rakukin extended his neck even more and again began an extremely rapid blinking of the eyes.

Pakin said:

– If you, Rakukin, don't stop that blinking immediately, I'll give you a good boot in the chest.

Rakukin, so as not to blink, twisted his jaws, extended his neck still further, and threw his head back.

– Uh, what an execrable sight you are – said Pakin. A mug like a chicken's, a blue neck, simply revolting.

At that instant, Rakukin's head was lolling back further and further and, finally, all tension lost, it collapsed on to his back.

– What the devil! exclaimed Pakin – What sort of a conjuring trick is that supposed to be?

Looking at Rakukin from Pakin's position, it could quite easily be assumed that Rakukin was sitting there with no head at all. Rakukin's Adam's apple was sticking up in the air. Unwittingly one might well think that it was his nose.

– Eh, Rakukin! – said Pakin.

Rakukin was silent!

– Rakukin! – repeated Pakin.

Rakukin didn't reply and continued to sit motionless.

– So – said Pakin – Rakukin's snuffed it.

Pakin crossed himself and left the room on tip-toe.

About fourteen minutes later a small soul climbed out of Rakukin's body and threw a malevolent look at the place where Pakin had just been sitting. But then the tall figure of the angel of death came out from behind the cupboard and, taking Rakukin's soul by the hand, led it away somewhere, straight through houses and walls. Rakukin's soul ran after the angel of death, constantly glancing malevolently back. But then the angel of death stepped up the pace and Rakukin's soul, leaping and stumbling, disappeared into space beyond the turning-point.

ASSORTED STORIES

[Kalindov]

Kalindov was standing on tiptoe and peering at me straight in the face. I found this unpleasant. I turned aside but Kalindov ran round me and was again peering at me straight in the face. I tried shielding myself from Kalindov with a newspaper. But Kalindov outwitted me: he set my newspaper alight and, when it flared up, I dropped it on the floor and Kalindov again began peering at me straight in the face. Slowly retreating, I repaired behind the cupboard and there, for a few moments, I enjoyed a break from the importunate stares of Kalindov. But my break was not prolonged: Kalindov crawled up to the cupboard on all fours and peered up at me from below. My patience ran out; I screwed up my eyes and booted Kalindov in the face.

When I opened my eyes, Kalindov was standing in front of me, his mug bloodied and mouth lacerated, peering at me straight in the face as before.

(1930)

Five Unfinished Narratives

Dear Yakov Semyonovich,
1. A certain man, having taken a run, struck his head against a smithy with such force that the blacksmith put aside the

sledge-hammer which he was holding, took off his leather apron and, having smoothed his hair with his palm, went out on to the street to see what had happened. 2. Then the smith spotted the man sitting on the ground. The man was sitting on the ground and holding his head. 3. – What happened? – asked the smith. – Ooh! – said the man. 4. The smith went a bit closer to the man. 5. We discontinue the narrative about the smith and the unknown man and begin a new narrative about four friends and a harem. 6. Once upon a time there were four harem fanatics. They considered it rather pleasant to have eight women at a time each. They would gather of an evening and debate harem life. They drank wine; they drank themselves blind drunk; they collapsed under the table; they puked up. It was disgusting to look at them. They bit each other on the leg. They bandied obscenities at each other. They crawled about on their bellies. 7. We discontinue the story about them and begin a new story about beer. 8. There was a barrel of beer and next to it sat a philosopher who contended: – This barrel is full of beer; the beer is fermenting and strengthening. And I in my mind ferment along the starry summits and strengthen my spirit. Beer is a drink flowing in space; I also am a drink, flowing in time. 9. When beer is enclosed in a barrel, it has nowhere to flow. Time will stop and I will stand up. 10. But if time does not stop, then my flow is immutable. 11. No, it's better to let the beer flow freely, for it's contrary to the laws of nature for it to stand still. – And with these words the philosopher turned on the tap in the barrel and the beer poured out over the floor. 12. We have related enough about beer; now we shall relate about a drum. 13. A philosopher beat a drum and shouted: – I am making a philosophical noise! This noise is of no use to anyone, it even annoys everyone. But if it annoys everyone, that means it is not of this world. And if it's not of this world, then it's from another world. And if it is from another world, then I shall keep making it. 14. The philosopher made his noise for a long time. But we shall leave this noisy story and turn to the following quiet story about trees. 15. A philosopher went for a walk under some trees and remained silent, because inspiration had deserted him.

(1931)

[Koka Briansky]

Act I

KOKA BRIANSKY	I'm getting married today.
MOTHER	What?
KOKA BRIANSKY	I'm getting married today.
MOTHER	What?
KOKA BRIANSKY	I said I'm getting married today.
MOTHER	What did you say?
KOKA BRIANSKY	To-day – ma-rried!
MOTHER	Ma? What's *ma*?
KOKA BRIANSKY	Ma-rri-age!
MOTHER	Idge? What's this idge?
KOKA BRIANSKY	Not idge, but ma-rri-age!
MOTHER	What do you mean, not idge?
KOKA BRIANSKY	Yes, not idge, that's all!
MOTHER	What?
KOKA BRIANSKY	Yes, not idge. Do you understand! Not idge!
MOTHER	You're on about that idge again. I don't know what idge's got to do with it.
KOKA BRIANSKY	Oh blow you! *Ma* and *idge*! What's up with

	you? Don't you realize yourself that saying just *ma* is senseless.
MOTHER	What did you say?
KOKA BRIANSKY	*Ma*, I said, is *senseless*!!!
MOTHER	sle?
KOKA BRIANSKY	What on earth is all this! How can you possibly manage to catch only bits of words, and only the most absurd bits at that: sle! Why sle in particular?
MOTHER	There you go again – sle.

KOKA BRIANSKY *throttles his* MOTHER. *Enter his fiancée* MARUSIA.

(1933)

[Aleksey Tolstoy]

Ol'ga Forsh went up to Aleksey Tolstoy and did something. Aleksey Tolstoy also did something.

At this point Konstantin Fedin and Valentin Stenich leapt outside and got down to looking for a suitable stone. They didn't find a stone but they found a spade. Konstantin Fedin cracked Ol'ga Forsh one across the chops with this spade.

Then Aleksey Tolstoy stripped off and, going out on to the Fontanka, began to neigh like a horse. Everyone said: – There goes a major contemporary writer, neighing. – And nobody touched Aleksey Tolstoy.

(1934)

On Phenomena and Existences

No. 1

The artist Michelangelo sits down on a heap of bricks and, propping his head in his hands, begins to think. Suddenly a cockerel walks past and looks at the artist Michelangelo with his round, golden eyes. Looks, but doesn't blink. At this point, the artist Michelangelo raises his head and sees the cockerel. The cockerel does not lower his gaze, doesn't blink and doesn't move his tail. The artist Michelangelo looks down and is aware of something in his eye. The artist Michelangelo rubs his eyes with his hands. And the cockerel isn't standing there any more, isn't standing there, but is walking away, walking away behind the shed, behind the shed to the poultry-run, to the poultry-run towards his hens.

And the artist Michelangelo gets up from the heap of bricks, shakes the red brick dust from his trousers, throws aside his belt and goes off to his wife.

The artist Michaelangelo's wife, by the way, is extremely long, all of two rooms in length.

On the way, the artist Michelangelo meets Komarov, grasps him by the hand and shouts: – Look! ...

Komarov looks and sees a sphere.

– What's that? – whispers Komarov.

And from the sky comes a roar: – It's a sphere.

– What sort of a sphere is it? – whispers Komarov.

And from the sky, the roar: – A smooth-surfaced sphere!

Komarov and the artist Michelangelo sit down on the grass and they are seated on the grass like mushrooms. They hold each other's hands and look up at the sky. And in the sky appears the outline of a huge spoon. What on earth is that? No one knows. People run about and lock themselves into their houses. They lock their doors and their windows. But will that really help? Much good it does them! It will not help.

I remember in 1884 an ordinary comet the size of a steamer appearing in the sky. It was very frightening. But now – a spoon! Some phenomenon for a comet!

Lock your windows and doors!

Can that really help? You can't barricade yourself with planks against a celestial phenomenon.

Nikolay Ivanovich Stupin lives in our house. He has a theory that everything is smoke. But in my view not everything is smoke. Maybe even there's no smoke at all. Maybe there's really nothing. There's one category only. Or maybe there's no category at all. It's hard to say.

It is said that a certain celebrated artist scrutinized a cockerel. He scrutinized it and scrutinized it and came to the conclusion that the cockerel did not exist.

The artist told his friend this, and his friend just laughed. How, he said, doesn't it exist, he said, when it's standing right here and I, he said, am clearly observing it.

And the great artist thereupon hung his head and, retaining the same posture in which he stood, sat down on a pile of bricks.

That's all.

Daniil Dandan, 18 September 1934

On Phenomena and Existences

No. 2

Here's a bottle of vodka, of the lethal spirit variety. And beside it you see Nikolay Ivanovich Serpukhov.

From the bottle rise spirituous fumes. Look at the way Nikolay Ivanovich Serpukhov is breathing them in through his nose. Mark how he licks his lips and how he screws up his eyes. Evidently he is particularly partial to it and, in the main, that's because it's that lethal spirit variety.

But take note of the fact that behind Nikolay Ivanovich's back there is nothing. It's not that there isn't a cupboard there, or a chest of drawers, or at any rate some such object: but there is absolutely nothing there, not even air. Believe it or not, as you please, but behind Nikolay Ivanovich's back there is not even an airless expanse or, as they say, universal ether. To put it bluntly, there's nothing.

This is, of course, utterly inconceivable.

But we don't give a damn about that, as we are only interested in the vodka and Nikolay Ivanovich Serpukhov.

And so Nikolay Ivanovich takes the bottle of vodka in his hand and puts it to his nose. Nikolay Ivanovich sniffs it and moves his mouth like a rabbit.

Now the time has come to say that, not only behind Nikolay Ivanovich's back, but before him too – as it were, in front of his chest – and all the way round him, there is nothing. A complete absence of any kind of existence, or, as the old witticism goes, an absence of any kind of presence.

However, let us interest ourselves only in the vodka and Nikolay Ivanovich.

Just imagine, Nikolay Ivanovich peers into the bottle of vodka, then he puts it to his lips, tips back the bottle bottom-end up, and knocks it back – just imagine it, the whole bottle.

Nifty! Nikolay Ivanovich knocked back his vodka and looked blank. Nifty, all right! How could he!

And now this is what we have to say: as a matter of fact, not only behind Nikolay Ivanovich's back, nor merely in front and all around him, but also even inside Nikolay Ivanovich there was nothing, nothing existed.

Of course, it could all be as we have just said, and yet Nikolay Ivanovich himself could in these circumstances still be in a delightful state of existence. This is, of course, true. But, as a matter of fact, the whole thing is that Nikolay Ivanovich didn't exist and doesn't exist. That's exactly the whole thing.

You may ask: and what about the bottle of vodka? In particular, where did the vodka go, if a non-existent Nikolay Ivanovich drank it? Let's say that the bottle remained. Where, then, is the vodka? There it was and, suddenly, there it isn't. We know Nikolay Ivanovich doesn't exist, you say. So, what's the explanation?

At this stage, we ourselves become lost in conjecture.

But, anyway, what are we talking about? Surely we said that inside, as well as outside, Nikolay Ivanovich nothing exists. So if, both inside and outside, nothing exists, then that means that the bottle as well doesn't exist. Isn't that it?

But, on the other hand, take note of the following: if we are saying that nothing exists either inside or outside, then the question arises: inside and outside of what? Something evidently, all the same, does exist? Or perhaps doesn't exist. In which case, why do we keep saying 'inside' and 'outside'?

No, here we have patently reached an impasse. And we ourselves don't know what to say.

Goodbye for now.

Daniil Dandan, 18 September 1934

On Equilibrium

Everyone now knows how dangerous swallowing stones is. A friend of mine even coined the expression 'Dan-ex-ston', which means: 'It's dangerous to extract stones.' And a good thing too. 'Dan-ex-ston' can be easily remembered and, as required, instantly recalled.

He worked, this friend of mine, as a stoker on a steam-engine. He travelled either the northern line or to Moscow. He was called Nikolay Ivanovich Serpukhov and he smoked Rocket cigarettes at thirty-five kopecks a packet, and always said that they made him cough less, while those costing five roubles, he says, 'always make me choke'.

And so Nikolay Ivanovich once chanced to get in to the restaurant in the Yevropeyskaya Hotel. Nikolay Ivanovich sat at a table and at the next table some foreigners were sitting munching apples.

At this point Nikolay Ivanovich said to himself: – This is interesting – said Nikolay Ivanovich – A man's life this!

Barely had he said this to himself when from out of the blue a Fairy appeared in front of him, saying: – My good man, what do you need?

Well, of course, in a restaurant you do get a commotion from which, it may be said, this unknown diminutive lady may have sprung. The foreigners even ceased munching their apples.

Nikolay Ivanovich himself rather had the wind up and spoke rather off-handedly, so as to give her the brush-off – I'm sorry – he said – but I don't really require anything in particular.

– You don't understand – said the unknown lady – I – she said – am what is called a Fairy. In the merest jiffy I'll lay on whatever you fancy.

Nikolay Ivanovich happened to notice that a citizen in a grey two-piece was listening intently to their conversation. The *maître d'hotel* was rushing through the open doors and behind him some other specimen with a cigarette in his mouth.

– Bloody hell! – thought Nikolay Ivanovich – there's no telling what's going on.

And there was indeed no telling what was going on. The *maître d'hotel* was leaping around the tables, the foreigners were rolling up the carpets and generally the devil only knew what! They were all doing whatever they felt like!

Nikolay Ivanovich ran out to the street and didn't even pick up his hat from the custody of the clockroom; he ran out on to Lassalle Street and said to himself: – Dan-ex-ston! It's dangerous to extract stones – Nothing like this ever really happens, surely!

And arriving home, Nikolay Ivanovich told his wife: – Don't be alarmed, Yekaterina Petrovna, and don't get worried. Only there's no equilibrium in the world. It's just an error of some kilogram and a half over the universe as a whole, but it's really a surprising thing, Yekaterina Petrovna, totally surprising!

And that's all.

Daniil Dandan, 18 September 1934

[Andrey Semyonovich]

Andrey Semyonovich spat into a cup of water. The water immediately turned black. Andrey Semyonovich screwed up his eyes and looked attentively into the cup. The water was very black. Andrey Semyonovich's heart began to throb.

At that moment Andrey Semyonovich's dog woke up. Andrey Semyonovich went over to the window and began ruminating.

Suddenly something big and dark shot past Andrey Semyonovich's face and flew out of the window. This was Andrey Semyonovich's dog flying out and it zoomed like a crow on to the roof of the building opposite. Andrey Semyonovich sat down on his haunches and began to howl.

Into the room ran Comrade Popugayev.

– What's up with you? Are you ill? – asked Comrade Popugayev.

Andrey Semyonovich quietened down and rubbed his eyes with his hands.

Comrade Popugayev took a look into the cup which was standing on the table. – What's this you've poured into here?

– he asked Andrey Semyonovich.

– I don't know – said Andrey Semyonovich.

Popugayev instantly disappeared. The dog flew in through the window again, lay down in its former place and went to sleep.

Andrey Semyonovich went over to the table and took a drink from the cup of blackened water. And Andrey Semyonovich's soul turned lucent.

(1934)

Rebellion

– Drink vinegar, gentlemen – said Shuyev.

No one gave him any reply.

– Gentlemen! – shouted Shuyev – I propose to you the drinking of vinegar!

Makaronov got up from his armchair and said: – I welcome Shuyev's idea. Let's drink vinegar.

Rastopyakin said: – I shall not be drinking vinegar.

At this point a silence set in and everyone began to look at Shuyev. Shuyev sat stony-faced. It was not clear what he was thinking.

Three minutes went by. Suchkov smothered a cough. Ryvin scratched his mouth. Kaltayev adjusted his tie. Makaronov jiggled his ears and his nose. And Rastopyakin, slumped against the back of his armchair, was looking as if indifferently into the fireplace.

Seven or eight more minutes went by.

Ryvin stood up and went out of the room on tiptoe.

Kaltayev followed him with his eyes.

When the door had closed behind Ryvin, Shuyev said: – So. The rebel has departed. To the devil with the rebel!

Everyone looked at each other in surprise, and Rastopyakin raised his head and fixed his gaze on Shuyev.

Shuyev said sternly: – He who rebels is a scoundrel!

Suchkov cautiously, under the table, shrugged his shoulders.

– I am in favour of the drinking of vinegar – Makaronov said quietly and looked expectantly at Shuyev.

Rastopyakin hiccupped and, with embarrassment, blushed like a maiden.

– Death to the rebels! – shouted Suchkov, baring his blackish teeth.

(1934?)

[Ivan Yakovlevich Bobov]

Ivan Yakovlevich Bobov woke up in the best possible of moods. He looked out from under his blanket and immediately spotted the ceiling. The ceiling was decorated with a large grey stain with greenish edges. If one looked closely at the stain, with one eye, then the stain took on a resemblance to a rhinoceros harnessed to a wheelbarrow, although others held that it looked more like a tram with a giant sitting on top – however, it was possible to detect in this stain even the outlines of some city or other. Ivan Yakovlevich looked at the ceiling, though not at where the stain was, but just like that, at no particular place; while doing so, he smiled and screwed up his eyes. Then he goggled his eyes and raised his eyebrows so high that his forehead folded up like a concertina and would very nearly have disappeared altogether if Ivan Yakovlevich had not screwed up his eyes again and suddenly, as though ashamed of something, pulled the blanket back up over his head. He did this so quickly that from under the other end of the blanket Ivan Yakovlevich's bare feet were exposed and right then a fly settled on the big toe of his left foot. Ivan Yakovlevich moved this toe and the fly flew over and settled on his heel. Then Ivan Yakovlevich grabbed the blanket with both feet; with one foot he hooked the blanket downwards, while he wiggled his other foot and clasped the blanket upwards with it and by this means pulled the blanket down from over his head. 'Up yours', said Ivan Yakovlevich and blew out his cheeks. Usually, whenever Ivan Yakovlevich managed to do something or, on the contrary, utterly failed, Ivan Yakovlevich always said 'up yours' – of course, not loudly and not at all so that anyone should hear it, but just like that, quietly to himself. And so, having said 'up yours', Ivan Yakovlevich sat on the bed and extended an arm to the chair, on which his trousers, shirt and underwear lay. As for trousers, Ivan Yakovlevich loved to wear striped ones. But, at one time, there was really a situation when it was impossible to get striped trousers anywhere. Ivan Yakovlevich tried 'Leningrad Clothes', and the department store, and the Passage, and Gostinyy Dvor and he had been round all the shops on the Petrograd side. He had even gone over to somewhere on Okhta but didn't find any striped trousers anywhere. And Ivan Yakovlevich's old trousers had worn so threadbare that it was getting impossible to wear them. Ivan Yakovlevich sewed them up several times but in the end even this didn't help any more. Ivan Yakovlevich again went round all the shops and, again not finding striped trousers anywhere, finally decided to buy checked ones. But checked trousers weren't available anywhere either. Then Ivan Yakovlevich decided to buy himself grey trousers, but he couldn't find grey ones anywhere either. Neither were black trousers in Ivan Yakovlevich's size anywhere to be found. Then Ivan Yakovlevich went off to buy blue trousers but, while he had been looking for black ones, both blue and brown ones also ran out. And so, finally, Ivan Yakovlevich just had to buy some green trousers with yellow spots. In the shop it had seemed to Ivan Yakovlevich that the trousers were not of a very bright colour and that the yellow fleck did not offend the eye at all. But, arriving home, Ivan Yakovlevich discovered that one leg was indeed of a decent shade but that the other was nothing short of turquoise and the yellow fleck positively flamed on it. Ivan Yakovlevich tried turning the trousers inside out, but that way round both legs had a propensity to assume a yellow hue embroidered with green peas and were so garish that, well, just to step out on stage in such trousers after a cinematic show would be quite sufficient: the audience would guffaw for half an hour. For two days Ivan Yakovlevich couldn't bring himself to put on his new trousers, but when his old ones got so torn that even from a distance it could be seen that Ivan Yakovlevich's underpants were in dire need of mending, there was nothing for it but to sport the new trousers. In his new trousers for the first time, Ivan Yakovlevich went out extremely cautiously. Leaving the doorway, he glanced both ways first and, having convinced himself that there was no one nearby, stepped out on to the street and swiftly strode off in the direction of his office. The first person he met was an apple seller with a big basket on his head. He said nothing on catching sight of Ivan Yakovlevich and only when Ivan Yakovlevich had walked past did he stop and, since his basket would not allow him to turn his head, the apple seller turned his whole person and followed Ivan Yakovlevich with his eyes – and perhaps would have shaken his head if, once again, it had not been for that same basket. Ivan Yakovlevich stepped it out jauntily, considering his encounter with the fruit seller to have been a good omen. He had not seen the tradesman's manoeuvre and he reassured himself that his trousers were not as startling as all that. There now walked towards Ivan Yakovlevich an office worker of just the same type as he himself, with a briefcase under his arm. The office worker was walking briskly, not bothering to look around him, but rather keeping a close watch underfoot. Drawing level with Ivan Yakovlevich, the office worker stole a glance at Ivan Yakovlevich's trousers and stopped in his tracks. Ivan Yakovlevich stopped as well. The office worker looked at Ivan Yakovlevich, as did Ivan Yakovlevich at the office worker.

– Excuse me – said the office worker – you couldn't tell me how to get to the ... national ... exchange?

– To get there you'll have to go along this footpath ... along this footbridge ... no, I mean, you'll have to go this way and then that way – said Ivan Yakovlevich.

The office worker said thank you and quickly walked away, and Ivan Yakovlevich took a few steps forward but, seeing that now towards him came not a male office worker but a female one, he lowered his head and ran across to the other side of the street. Ivan Yakovlevich arrived at the office with some delay and very bad tempered. Ivan Yakovlevich's colleagues naturally focused their attention on the green trousers with legs of varying hue but, evidently guessing that this was the cause of his bad temper, they did not trouble him with questions. Ivan Yakovlevich underwent torture for two weeks wearing his green trousers, until one of his colleagues, one Apollon Maksimovich Shilov, suggested to Ivan Yakovlevich that he should buy a pair of striped trousers from Apollon Maksimovich himself which were ostensibly surplus to Apollon Maksimovich's requirements.

(1934–1937)

A Knight

Aleksey Alekseyevich Alekseyev was a real knight. So, for example, on one occasion, catching sight from a tram of a lady stumbling against a kerbstone and dropping from her bag a glass lampshade for a table-lamp, which promptly smashed, Aleksey Alekseyevich, desiring to help the lady, decided to sacrifice himself and, leaping from the tram at full speed, fell and split open the whole of his phizog on a stone. Another time, seeing a lady who was climbing over a fence catch her skirt on a nail and get stuck there, so that she could move neither backward nor forward, Aleksey Alekseyevich began to get so agitated that, in his agitation, he broke two front teeth with his tongue. In a word, Aleksey Alekseyevich was really the most chivalrous knight, and not only in relation to ladies. With unprecedented ease, Aleksey Alekseyevich could sacrifice his life for his Faith, Tsar and Fatherland, as he proved in the year '14, at the start of the German war, by throwing himself, with the cry 'For the Motherland!', on to the street from a second-floor window. By some miracle, Aleksey Alekseyevich remained alive, getting off with only light injuries, and was quickly, as such an uncommonly zealous patriot, dispatched to the front.

At the front, Aleksey Alekseyevich distinguished himself with his unprecedentedly elevated feelings and every time he pronounced the words 'banner', 'fanfare', or even just 'epaulettes', down his face there would trickle a tear of emotion.

In the year '16, Aleksey Alekseyevich was wounded in the loins and withdrew from the front.

As a first-category invalid, Aleksey Alekseyevich had no longer to serve and, profiting from the time on his hands, committed his patriotic feelings to paper.

Once, chatting to Konstantin Lebedev, Aleksey Alekseyevich came out with his favourite utterance – I have suffered for the motherland and wrecked my loins, but I exist by the strength of conviction in my posterior subconscious.

– And you're a fool! – said Konstantin Lebedev. – The highest service to the motherland is rendered only by a Liberal.

For some reason, these words became deeply imprinted on the mind of Aleksey Alekseyevich and so, in the year '17, he was already calling himself *a liberal whose loins had suffered for his native land.*

Aleksey Alekseyevich greeted the Revolution with delight, notwithstanding even the fact that he was deprived of his pension. For a certain time Konstantin Lebedev supplied him with cane-sugar, chocolate, preserved suet and millet groats. But when Konstantin Lebedev suddenly went missing no one knew where, Aleksey Alekseyevich had to take to the streets and ask for charity. At first, Aleksey Alekseyevich would extend his hand and say: – Give charity, for Christ's sake, to he whose loins have suffered for the motherland. – But this brought no success. Then Aleksey Alekseyevich changed the word 'motherland' to the word 'revolution'. But this too brought no success. Then Aleksey Alekseyevich composed a revolutionary song, and, if he saw on the street a person capable, in Aleksey Alekseyevich's opinion, of giving alms, he would take a step forward and proudly, with dignity, throw back his head and start singing:

> To the barricades
> We will all zoom!
> For freedom
> We will ourselves all maim and doom!

And, jauntily tapping his heels in the Polish manner, Aleksey Alekseyevich would extend his hat and say – Alms, please, for Christ's sake. – This did help and Aleksey Alekseyevich rarely remained without food.

Everything was going well, but then, in the year '22, Aleksey Alekseyevich got to know a certain Ivan Ivanovich Puzyryov, who dealt in sunflower oil in the Haymarket. Puzyryov invited Aleksey Alekseyevich to a café, treated him to real coffee and, himself chomping fancy cakes, expounded to him some sort of complicated enterprise of which Aleksey Alekseyevich understood only that he had to do something, in return for which he would receive from Puzyryov the most costly items of nutrition. Aleksey Alekseyevich agreed and Puzyryov, on the spot, as an incentive, passed him under the table two caddies of tea and a packet of Rajah cigarettes.

After this, Aleksey Alekseyevich came to see Puzyryov every morning at the market, and picking up from him some sort of papers with crooked signatures and numerous seals, took a sleigh, if it were winter and if it were summer a cart, and set off as instructed by Puzyryov, to do the rounds of various establishments where, producing the papers, he would receive some sort of boxes, which he would load on to his sleigh or cart, and in the evening take them to Puzyryov at his flat. But once, when Aleksey Alekseyevich had just rolled up in his sleigh at Puzyryov's flat, two men came up to him, one of whom was in a military great-coat, and asked him: – Is your name Alekseyev? – Then Aleksey Alekseyevich was put into an automobile and taken away to prison.

At the interrogation, Aleksey Alekseyevich understood not a thing and just kept saying that he had suffered for his revolutionary motherland. But, despite this, he was sentenced to ten years of exile in the northern parts of his fatherland. Having got back in the year '28 to Leningrad, Aleksey Alekseyevich began to ply his previous trade and, standing up on the corner of Volodarskiy, tossed back his head with dignity, tapped his heel and sang out:

To the barricades
We will all zoom!
For freedom
We will ourselves all maim and doom!

But he did not even manage to sing it through twice before he was taken away in a covered vehicle to somewhere in the direction of the Admiralty. His feet never touched the ground.

And there we have a short narrative of the life of the valiant knight and patriot, Aleksey Alekseyevich Alekseyev.

(1934–36)

A Story

Abram Demyanovich Pantopasov cried out loudly and pressed a handkerchief to his eyes. But it was too late. Ash and soft dush had gummed up Abram Demyanovich's eyes. From then on Abram Demyanovich's eyes began to hurt, they were gradually covered over with repulsive scabs, and Abram Demyanovich went blind.

As a blind invalid, Abram Demyanovich was given the push from his job and accorded a wretched pittance of thirty-six roubles a month.

Quite clearly this sum was insufficient for Abram Demyanovich to live on. A kilo of bread cost a rouble and ten kopecks, and a leek cost forty-eight kopecks at the market.

And so the industrial invalid began more and more to concentrate his attention on rubbish bins.

It was difficult for a blind man to find the edible scraps among all the peelings and filth.

Even finding the rubbish itself in someone else's yard is not easy. You can't see it with your eyes, and to ask – Whereabouts here is your rubbish bin? – is somehow a bit awkward.

The only way left is to sniff it out.

Some rubbish bins reek so much you can smell them a mile away, but others with lids are absolutely impossible to detect.

It's all right if you happen upon a kindly caretaker, but the other sort would so put the wind up you that you'd lose your appetite.

Once Abram Demyanovich climbed into someone's rubbish bin and when he was in there a rat bit him, and he climbed straight back out again. So that day he didn't eat anything.

But then one morning something jumped out of Abram Demyanovich's right eye.

Abram Demyanovich rubbed the eye and suddenly saw daylight. And then something jumped out of his left eye, too, and Abram Demyanovich saw the light.

From that day on it was all downhill for Abram Demyanovich.

Everywhere Abram Demyanovich was in great demand.

In the People's Committee for Heavy Industry office Abram Demyanovich was a minor sensation.

And so Abram Demyanovich became a great man.

(1935)

An Unexpected Drinking Bout

Once Antonina Alekseyevna struck her husband with her office stamp and imprinted his forehead with stamp-pad ink.

The mortally offended Pyotr Leonidovich, Antonina Alekseyevna's husband, locked himself in the bathroom and wouldn't let anyone in.

However, the residents of the communal flat, having a strong need to get in to where Pyotr Leonidovich was sitting, decided to break down the locked door by force.

Seeing that the game was up, Pyotr Leonidovich came out of the bathroom and, going back into his own flat, lay down on the bed.

But Antonina Alekseyevna decided to persecute her husband to the limit. She tore up little bits of paper and showered them on to Pyotr Leonidovich who was lying on the bed.

The infuriated Pyotr Leonidovich leaped out into the corridor and set about tearing the wallpaper.

At this point all the residents ran out and, seeing what the hapless Pyotr Leonidovich was doing, they threw themselves on to him and ripped the waistcoat that he was wearing.

Pyotr Leonidovich ran off to the porter's office.

During this time, Antonina Alekseyevna had stripped naked and had hidden in the trunk.

Ten minutes later Pyotr Leonidovich returned, followed by the house manager.

Not finding his wife in the room, Pyotr Leonidovich with the house manager decided to take advantage of the empty premises in order to down some vodka. Pyotr Leonidovich undertook to run off to the corner for the said beverage.

When Pyotr Leonidovich had gone out, Antonina Alekseyevna climbed out of the trunk and appeared before the house manager in a state of nakedness.

The shaken house manager leaped from his chair and rushed up to the window, but, seeing the muscular build of the young twenty-six-year-old woman, he suddenly gave way to wild rapture.

At this point Pyotr Leonidovich returned with a litre of vodka.

Catching sight of what was afoot in his room, Pyotr Leonidovich knitted his brows.

But his spouse Antonina Alekseyevna showed him her office stamp and Pyotr Leonidovich calmed down.

Antonina Alekseyevna expressed a desire to participate in the drinking session, but strictly on condition that she maintain her naked state and, to boot, that she sit on the table on which it was proposed to set out the snacks to accompany the vodka.

The men sat down on chairs, Antonina Alekseyevna sat on the table and the drinking commenced.

It cannot be called hygienic if a naked young woman is sitting on the very table at which people are eating. Moreover Antonina Alekseyevna was a woman of a rather plump build and not all that particular about her bodily cleanliness, so it was a pretty devilish state of affairs.

Soon, however, they had all drunk themselves into a stupor and fallen asleep: the men on the floor and Antonina Alekseyevna on the table.

And silence was established in the communal flat.

(1935)

Theme for a Story

A certain engineer has made up his mind to build a huge brick wall across Petersburg. He considers how to accomplish this, doesn't sleep for nights cogitating it. Gradually a group of engineering planners is formed and a plan for the construction of the wall is elaborated. It was decided to build the wall at night, indeed, to build the whole thing in one night, so that it would appear as a surprise to everyone. Workers are summoned. The organization is under way. The city authorities are sidelined and finally the night arrives when this wall is to be built. The building of the wall is known only to four men. The workers and engineers receive exact instructions as to whom to place where and what to do. Thanks to exact calculation, they succeed in putting up the wall in a single night. On the following day there is consternation in Petersburg. And the inventor of the wall is himself dejected. To what use this wall was to be put, he himself did not know.

(1935)

[There Once Was a Man ...]

There once was a man whose name was Kuznetsov. He left his house to go to a shop to buy some carpenter's glue so as to stick a stool.

When Kuznetsov was walking past an unfinished house, a brick fell off the top and hit Kuznetsov on the head.

Kuznetsov fell, but straight away jumped to his feet and felt over his head. On Kuznetsov's head a huge lump had come up.

Kuznetsov gave the lump a rub and said: — I, citizen Kuznetsov, left the house to go to the shop to ... to ... to ... Oh, what on earth's happened? I've forgotten why I was going to the shop!

At this point a second brick fell off the roof and again Kuznetsov was struck on the head.

— Akh! — cried Kuznetsov, clutching at his head and feeling a second lump on his head.

— A likely story! — said Kuznetsov. — I, citizen Kuznetsov, left the house to go to ... to go to ... to go to ... where was I going!

Then a third brick fell from the top on to Kuznetsov's head. And on Kuznetsov's head a third lump came up.

– Oh heck! – yelled out Kuznetsov, snatching at his head. – I, citizen Kuznetsov, left the . . . left the . . . left the cellar? No. Left the boozer? No! Where did I leave?

A fourth brick fell from the roof, hit Kuznetsov on the back of the head and a fourth lump came up on Kuznetsov.

– Well, now then! – said Kuznetsov, scratching the back of his head. – I . . . I . . . I . . . Who am I? I seem to have forgotten what my name is . . . A likely story! Whatever's my name? Vasily Petukhov? No. Nikolay Sapogov? No. Panteley Rysakov? No. Well, who the hell am I?

But then a fifth brick fell off the roof and so struck Kuznetsov on the back of the head that Kuznetsov forgot everything once and for all and, crying 'Oh, oh, oh!', ran off down the street.

If you wouldn't mind! If anyone should meet a man in the street with five lumps on his head, please remind him that his name is Kuznetsov and that he has to buy some carpenter's glue and repair a broken stool.

(1935)

Father and Daughter

Natasha had two sweets. Then she ate one of the sweets and one sweet remained. Natasha placed the sweet on the table in front of her and started crying.

Suddenly she has a look and on the table in front of her there lie two sweets again.

Natasha ate one sweet and again started crying.

Natasha cries and keeps one eye on the table to see whether a second sweet will appear. But a second sweet did not appear.

Natasha stopped crying and started to sing. She sang and sang away, and suddenly died.

Natasha's Dad arrived, took Natasha and carried her to the house manager.

– Here – says Natasha's Dad – will you witness the death?

The house manager blew on his stamp and applied it to Natasha's forehead.

– Thank you – said Natasha's Dad and carried Natasha off to the cemetery.

But at the cemetery was the watchman Matvei; he always sat by the gate and didn't let anyone into the cemetery, so that the dead had to be buried right on the street.

Dad buried Natasha on the street, removed his cap, placed it on the spot where he had interred Natasha and went off home.

He arrived home and Natasha was already sitting there. How come? It's very simple: she climbed out from under the earth and ran back home.

What a thing! Dad was so taken aback that he collapsed and died.

Natasha called the house manager, saying to him: – Will you witness a death?

The house manager blew on his stamp and applied it to a sheet of paper and then on the same sheet of paper he wrote: 'This certifies that so and so has actually died.'

Natasha took the piece of paper and carried it off to the cemetery for burial. But the watchman Matvei tells Natasha: – I'm not letting you in on any account.

Natasha says: – I just want to bury this piece of paper.

And the watchman says: – Don't even ask.

Natasha interred the piece of paper on the street, placed her socks on the spot where she had interred the piece of paper and went off home.

She gets home and Dad is already sitting there at home and is already playing against himself on a miniature billiard table with little metal balls.

Natasha was surprised but said nothing and went off to her room to grow up.

She grew and grew and within four years she had become a grown-up young lady. But Natasha's Dad had become aged and bent. But they will both remember how they had taken each other for dead and so they will fall on the divan and just laugh. Another time they laugh for about twenty minutes.

And their neighbours, as soon as they hear this laughter, immediately put on their coats and go off to the cinema. And one day they went off like that and never came back again. Seemingly, they were run over by a car.

(1936)

The Fate of a Professor's Wife

Once a certain professor ate something which didn't agree with him and he began to vomit.

His wife came up to him, saying: – What is it?

But the professor replied: – It's nothing. – His wife retreated again.

The professor reclined on the divan, had a little lie down, felt rested and went off to work. At work there was a surprise for him: his salary had been docked; instead of 650 roubles, he only had 500. The professor ran hither and thither – but to no avail. The professor went to the Director, and the Director threw him out. The professor went to the accountant, and the accountant said: – Apply to the Director. – The professor got on a train and went off to Moscow.

On the way the professor went down with flu. He arrived in Moscow and couldn't get out on to the platform.

They put the professor on a stretcher and carried him off to hospital.

The professor lay in hospital no more than four days and then died.

The professor's body was cremated, the ashes were placed in an urn and sent off to his wife.

So the professor's wife was sitting drinking coffee. Suddenly a ring. What's that? – A parcel for you.

The professor's wife was really pleased; smiling all over her face, she thrust a tip into the postman's hand and was soon unwrapping the parcel.

She looked in the parcel and saw an urn of ashes, with a message: 'Herewith all that remains of your spouse.'

The professor's wife didn't understand a thing; she shook the urn, held it up to the light, read the message six times – finally she worked out what was afoot and was terribly upset.

The professor's wife was very upset, cried for three hours and then went off to inter the urn of ashes. She wrapped the urn in a newspaper and took it to the First Five-Year Plan Garden, formerly the Tavricheskiy.

The professor's wife chose the most out-of-the-way path and was just intending to bury the urn, when suddenly a watchman came along.

– Hey! – shouted the watchman. – What are you doing here?

The professor's wife was frightened and said: — I just wanted to catch some frogs in this jar.

— Well — said the watchman — that's all right, only watch it, and keep off the grass.

When the watchman had gone, the professor's wife buried the urn, trod the earth down around it and went off for a stroll round the gardens.

In the gardens, she was accosted by some sailor — Come on, let's go for a little sleep — he said.

She replied: — Why should one sleep in the daytime? — But he stuck to his guns: sleep and more sleep.

And the professor's wife really did feel like sleeping.

She walked along the streets and she felt sleepy. People were running all around her in blue, or in green — and she just felt sleepy.

So she walked and slept. And she dreamed that Lev Tolstoy was coming towards her, holding a chamber-pot in his hands. She asked him: — What's that, then? — and he pointed to the chamber-pot, saying: — Here, I've really done something and now I'm taking it to show the whole world. Let everyone see it — he said.

The professor's wife also had a look and saw that it seemed no longer to be Tolstoy, but a shed, and in the shed was a hen.

The professor's wife tried to catch the hen, but the hen hid under a divan, from which it looked out, now in the form of a rabbit.

The professor's wife crawled under the divan after the rabbit and woke up.

She woke and looked around: she really was lying under a divan.

The professor's wife crawled out from under the divan — and saw her own room. And there stood the table with her undrunk coffee. On the table lay the message — Herewith all that remains of your spouse.

The professor's wife shed a few more tears and sat down to drink up her cold coffee.

Suddenly a ring. What's that? Some people walk in and say – Let's go.

– Where? – asked the professor's wife.

– To the lunatic asylum – they reply.

The professor's wife began to shout and to dig in her heels, but the people grabbed her and took her off to the lunatic asylum.

And there, on a bunk in a lunatic asylum, sits a completely normal professor's wife, holding a fishing rod and fishing on the floor for some invisible fish or other.

This professor's wife is merely a pitiful example of how many unfortunates there are in life who do not occupy in life the position that they ought to occupy.

(1936)

The Cashier

Masha found a mushroom, picked it and took it to the market. At the market, Masha was hit about the head, and there were further promises that she could be hit about the legs as well. Masha took fright and ran off.

Masha ran to the co-operative store and wanted to hide there behind the cash desk. But the manager caught sight of Masha and said: – What's that you've got in your hands?

And Masha said: – A mushroom.

The manager said: – Why, you're a fine one, now! How would you like me to fix you up with a job?

– Oh, you won't fix me up – said Masha.

– I'll fix you up here and now! – said the manager. And he fixed Masha up with a job, turning the handle on the cash till.

Masha turned and turned away on the handle on the cash till and suddenly died. The police arrived, drew up a report, and ordered the manager to pay a fine of fifteen roubles.

– What's the fine for? – asked the manager.

– For murder – replied the police.

The manager took fright, hastily paid the fine and said: – All right, only take this dead cashier out of here straight away.

At this point the sales assistant from the fruit section said: – No, wait a minute, you've got it wrong, she wasn't the cashier. She only turned the handle on the cash till. That's the cashier sitting there.

– It's all the same to us – said the police – we've been told to take a cashier out of here, so we'll take one out.

The police started towards the cashier. The cashier thereupon lay down on the floor behind the cash desk and said: – I won't go.

– Why won't you go, you silly woman? – said the police.

– You're going to bury me alive – said the cashier.

The police started to try and lift the cashier up from the floor, but try as they might, they couldn't lift her, as she was extremely stout.

– Grab her by the legs – said the sales assistant from the fruit section.

– No – said the manager – this cashier acts as my wife. I must therefore ask you not to expose her from the rear end.

– Do you hear? – said the cashier – don't you dare expose me from the rear end.

The police took hold of the cashier under the arms and

dragged and heaved her out of the co-operative store.

The manager ordered the sales assistants to tidy up the store and get business under way.

– But what are we going to do with this dead woman? – said the sales assistant from the fruit section, pointing at Masha.

– Good gracious me – said the manager – we've made a mess of the whole thing! Well, what in fact are we going to do with the dead woman?

– And who's going to sit at the cash till? – asked the sales assistant.

The manager clutched his head with both hands. He sent apples scattering along the counter with his knee and said: – What's happened is monstrous!

– Monstrous! – echoed the sales assistants in chorus.

Suddenly the manager scratched his moustache and said: – Ha, ha, I'm not so easily nonplussed. We'll seat the dead woman behind the till, and perhaps the public won't realize who's sitting there.

They seated the dead woman at the cash desk, stuck a cigarette between her teeth to give her a greater resemblance to the living, and for additional verisimilitude gave her the mushroom to hold in her hands.

The dead woman sat there looking quite alive, except that her facial colouring was very green, and one eye was open, while the other was completely closed.

– Never mind – said the manager – she'll do.

And the public was already knocking at the doors, highly agitated that the shop had not been opened. In particular, one matriarchal figure in a silk coat was shouting her head off: she was shaking her purse and aiming a back heel kick at the door-handle. And behind the matriarchal figure some old woman with a pillowcase on her head was shouting and swearing, calling the manager of the co-operative store a stingy old swine.

The manager opened the doors and admitted the public. The public charged straight to the meat section, and then to where the sugar and pepper were sold. But the old woman made straight for the fish section, and on the way glanced at the cashier and stopped.

– Good Lord – she said – Holy goats!

And the matriarchal figure in the silk coat had already been round every section, and was rushing to the cash desk. But no sooner had she glimpsed the cashier then she stopped dead, stood in silence and just looked. And the sales assistants also stayed silent and looked at the manager. And the manager peered out from behind the counter, waiting to see what would happen next.

The matriarchal figure in the silk coat turned to the sales assistants and said: – Who's that you've got sitting behind the cash till?

And the sales assistants stayed silent, as they didn't know what to say.

The manager also stayed silent.

At this point people came running from all sides. Already there was a crowd on the street. Caretakers from nearby houses appeared on the scene. Whistles were heard blowing. In a word, an absolute scandal.

The crowd was prepared to stand there outside the store until evening at least. But someone said that old women were plummeting out of a window on Ozerniy Pereulok. Then the crowd outside the store thinned out, because a lot of people went over to Ozerniy Pereulok.

(1936)

The Memoirs of a Wise Old Man

I used to be a very wise old man.

Now I am not quite right; you may consider me even not to exist at all. But the time was when any one of you would have come to me and, whatever burden may have oppressed a person, whatever sins may have tormented his thoughts, I would have embraced him and said: – My son, take comfort, for no burden is oppressing you and I see no bodily sins in you – and he would scamper away from me in happiness and joy.

I was great and strong. People who met me on the street would shy to one side and I would pass through a crowd like a flat iron.

My feet would often be kissed, but I didn't protest: I knew I deserved it. Why deprive people of the pleasure of honouring me? I myself, being extraordinarily lithe of body, even tried to kiss myself on my own foot. I sat on a bench, got hold of my right foot and pulled it up to my face. I managed to kiss the big toe. I was happy. I understood the happiness of others.

Everyone worshipped me! And not only people, but even beasts, while even various insects crawled before me and wagged their tails. And cats! They simply adored me and, somehow or other gripping each other's paws, would run in front of me whenever I was on the staircase.

At that time I was indeed very wise and understood everything. There was not a thing that would nonplus me. Just a minute's exertion of my colossal mind and the most complicated question would be resolved in the simplest possible manner. I was even taken to the Brain Institute and shown off to the learned professors. They measured my mind by electricity and simply boggled. – We have never seen anything like it – they said.

I was married, but rarely saw my wife. She was afraid of me: the enormity of my mind overwhelmed her. She did not so much live, as tremble; and if I as much as looked at her, she would begin to hiccup. We lived together for a long time, but then I think she disappeared somewhere. I don't remember exactly.

Memory – that's a strange thing altogether. How hard remembering is, and how easy forgetting! That's how it often is: you memorize one thing, and then remember something entirely different. Or: you memorize something with some difficulty, but very thoroughly, and then you can't remember anything. That also happens. I would advise everyone to work a bit on their memory.

I always believed in fair play and never beat anyone for no reason, because, when you are beating someone, you always go a bit daft and you might overdo it. Children, for example, should never be beaten with a knife or with anything made of iron, but women – the opposite: they shouldn't be kicked. Animals – they, it is said, have more endurance. But I have carried out experiments in this line and I know that this is not always the case.

Thanks to my litheness, I was able to do things which no one else could do. For example, I managed to retrieve by hand from an extremely sinuous sewage pipe my brother's earring, which had accidently fallen there. I could, for example, hide in a comparatively small basket and put the lid on myself.

Yes, certainly, I was phenomenal!

My brother was my complete opposite: in the first place, he was taller and, secondly, more stupid.

He and I were never very friendly. Although, however, we were friendly, even very. I've got something wrong here: to be exact, he and I were not friendly and were always on bad terms. And this is how he and I fell out. I was standing beside a shop: they were issuing sugar there, and I was standing in the queue, trying not to listen to what was being said around me. I had slight toothache and was not in the greatest of moods. It was very cold outside, because everyone was standing in quilted fur coats and they were still freezing. I was also standing in a quilted fur, but I was not freezing myself, though my hands were freezing because I had to keep taking them out of my pockets to adjust the suitcase I was holding between my knees, so that it didn't go missing. Suddenly someone struck me on the back. I flew into a state of indescribable indignation and, like greased lightning, began to consider how to punish the offender. During this time, I was struck a second time on the back. I pricked up my ears, but decided against turning my head and pretended that I hadn't noticed. I just, to be on the safe side, took the suitcase in my hand. Seven minutes passed and I was struck on the back a third time. At this I turned round and saw in front of me a tall middle-aged man in a rather shabby, but still quite good, military fur coat.

– What do you want from me? – I asked him in strict and even slightly metallic voice.

– And you, why don't you turn when you're called? – he said.

I had begun to think over the content of his words when he again opened his mouth and said: – What's wrong with you? Don't you recognize me or something? I'm your brother.

I again began to think over his words when he again opened his mouth and said: – Just listen, brother mine. I'm four roubles short for the sugar and it's a nuisance to have to leave the queue. Lend me five and I'll settle up with you later.

I started to ponder why my brother should be four roubles short, but he grabbed hold of my sleeve and said: — Well, so then, are you going to lend your own brother some money? — and with these words he undid my quilted fur for me himself, got into my inside pocket and reached my purse.

— Here we are — he said. — I'm taking a loan of a certain sum, and your purse, look, here it is, I'm putting back in your coat. — And he shoved my purse into the outer pocket of my fur.

I was of course surprised at meeting my brother so unexpectedly. For a while I was silent, and then I asked him: — But where have you been until now?

— There — replied my brother, waving in some direction or other.

I started thinking over where this 'there' might be, but my brother nudged me in the side and said: — Look, they've started letting us in to the shop.

We went together as far as the shop doors, but inside the shop I proved to be on my own, without my brother. Just for a moment, I jumped out of the queue and looked through the door on to the street. But there was no sign of my brother.

When I again wanted to take my place in the queue, they wouldn't let me in and even pushed me gradually out on to the street. Holding back my anger at such bad manners, I went off home. At home I discovered that my brother had taken all the money from my purse. At this stage I got absolutely furious with my brother, and since then he and I have never made it up.

I lived alone and granted admittance only to those who came to me for advice. But there were many of these and it turned out that I knew peace neither by day nor by night. Sometimes I would get so tired that I would lie down on the floor and rest. I would lie on the floor until I got cold; then I would jump up and start running round the room, to warm up. Then I would again sit down on the bench and give advice to all in need of it.

They would come in to me one after the other, sometimes not even opening the doors. I used to enjoy looking at their excruciating faces. I would talk to them, hardly able to stop myself laughing.

Once I couldn't contain myself and burst out laughing. They rushed in horror to escape – some through the door, some through the window, and some straight through the walls.

Left on my own, I drew myself up to my full majestic height, opened my mouth and said: – Prin tim pram.

But at this point something in me cracked and, since then, you might consider that I am no more.

(1936–38)

Comprehensive Research

YERMOLAYEV I have been at Blinov's and he gave me a demonstration of his strength. I've never seen anything like it. The strength of a wild animal! It was awful to behold. Blinov lifted up a writing table, swung it about and tossed it all of four metres away from him.

DOCTOR It would be interesting to research this phenomenon. Such facts are known to science, but the reasons for it are not understood. Where such muscular strength comes from, scientists are not yet able to say. Introduce me to Blinov. I'll give him a research pill.

YERMOLAYEV What sort of a pill is it that you are intending to give Blinov?

DOCTOR Pill? I don't intend to give him a pill.

YERMOLAYEV But you only just said yourself that you were intending to give him a pill.

DOCTOR No, no. You are mistaken. I didn't mention a pill.

YERMOLAYEV Well, excuse me, but I heard you mention a pill.

DOCTOR No.

YERMOLAYEV What do you mean – no?

DOCTOR I didn't say that.

YERMOLAYEV Who didn't say it?

DOCTOR You didn't say it.

YERMOLAYEV What didn't I say?

DOCTOR You, it seems to me, didn't finish saying something.

YERMOLAYEV I don't understand. What didn't I finish saying?

DOCTOR Your speech pattern is very typical. You swallow your words, you don't complete the utterance of your initial thought, you hurry and then you stutter.

YERMOLAYEV When did I stutter? I speak quite fluently.

DOCTOR Ah, but that's where you're wrong. Do you see? You're even starting to come out in red blotches from the tension. Your hands haven't gone cold yet?

YERMOLAYEV No, but so what?

DOCTOR Yes, that was my supposition. I think you're already having trouble breathing. You'd better

	sit down, before you fall down. That's right. Now have a rest.
YERMOLAYEV	But what for?
DOCTOR	Sh! Don't strain your vocal chords. Now I'm going to alleviate your fate.
YERMOLAYEV	Doctor! You frighten me.
DOCTOR	My dear friend! I want to help you. Here, take this. Swallow it!
YERMOLAYEV	Oh. Ooh! What a vile, disgusting taste! What is it you've given me?
DOCTOR	Nothing, it's all right. Calm down. It's a sure remedy.
YERMOLAYEV	I'm hot and everything seems to be turning green.
DOCTOR	Yes, that's right, my dear friend. In a minute, you'll die.
YERMOLAYEV	What are you saying? Doctor! Oh! I can't! Doctor! What have you given me? Oh, Doctor!
DOCTOR	You have swallowed the research pill.
YERMOLAYEV	Save me. Oh. Save me. Oh. Let me breathe. Oh. Save . . . Oh. Breathe . . .
DOCTOR	He's gone quiet. And he's not breathing. That means he's dead already. He has died, not finding on earth the answers to his questions. Yes, we physicians must comprehensively research the phenomenon of death.

(1937)

The Connection

Philosopher!

1. I am writing to you in reply to your letter, which you are intending to write to me in reply to my letter which I wrote to you.

2. A certain violinist bought himself a magnet and was taking it home. On the way some hooligans attacked the violinist and knocked his cap off. The wind caught his cap and carried it along the street.

3. The violinist put his magnet down and ran off after his cap. The cap landed in a puddle of nitric acid, where it decomposed.

4. And the hooligans had, by that time, grabbed the magnet and made off.

5. The violinist returned home without his coat and without his cap, because the cap had decomposed in the nitric acid and the violinist, distressed by the loss of his cap, had forgotten his coat on the tram.

6. The conductor of the tram in question took the coat to a second-hand shop and there he exchanged it for some sour cream, groats and tomatoes.

7. The conductor's father-in-law stuffed himself on the tomatoes and died. The conductor's father-in-law's body was placed in the morgue, but then things got mixed up and, instead of the conductor's father-in-law, they buried some old woman.

8. On the old woman's grave they placed a white post with the inscription: 'Anton Sergeyevich Kondrat'ev'.

9. Eleven years later, this post fell down, eaten through by

worms. And the cemetery watchman sawed the post into four pieces and burned it in his stove. And the cemetery watchman's wife cooked cauliflower soup over this fire.

10. But, when the soup was just ready, the clock fell off the wall right into the saucepan full of soup. They got the clock out of the soup, but there had been bedbugs in the clock and now they were in the soup. They gave the soup to Timofey the beggar.

11. Timofey the beggar ate the soup, bugs and all, and told Nikolay the beggar of the cemetery watchman's generosity.

12. The next day Nikolay the beggar went to the cemetery watchman and started asking him for alms. But the cemetery watchman didn't give Nikolay the beggar anything and chased him away.

13. Nikolay the beggar took this very badly and burned down the house of the cemetery watchman.

14. The fire spread from the house to the church and the church burned down.

15. A lengthy investigation took place, but the cause of the fire could not be established.

16. On the spot where the church had stood they built a club and on the club's opening day a concert was arranged, at which performed the violinist who, fourteen years before, had lost his coat.

17. And amid the audience there sat the son of one of those hooligans who, fourteen years before, had knocked the cap off this violinist.

18. After the concert they travelled home in the same tram. But, in the tram which was following theirs, the tram-driver was that very conductor who had once sold the violinist's coat at the second-hand shop.

19. And so there they are, travelling across the city in the late evening: in front are the violinist and the hooligan's son, and

behind them the tram-driver and former conductor.
20. They travel on and are not aware of what the connection is between them and this they will never learn until their dying day.

(1937)

A Nasty Character

Sen'ka bashed Fed'ka across the chops and hid under the chest of drawers.

Fed'ka got Sen'ka out from under the chest of drawers with a poker and tore off his right ear.

Sen'ka slipped through Fed'ka's hands and, holding his torn-off ear, ran off to the neighbours.

But Fed'ka caught up with Sen'ka and coshed him over the head with the sugar-basin.

Sen'ka collapsed and, seemingly, died.

Then Fed'ka packed his things in a suitcase and went away to Vladivostok.

In Vladivostok Fed'ka became a tailor; strictly speaking, he was not exactly a tailor, because he made only ladies' underwear, principally drawers and brassières. The ladies had no inhibitions with Fed'ka; right in front of him they would hitch up their skirts and Fed'ka would take their measurements.

Fed'ka, as one might say, didn't half see some sights.

Fed'ka was a nasty character.

Fed'ka was the murderer of Sen'ka.

Fed'ka was a lecherous devil.

Fed'ka was a glutton, because every evening he ate a dozen cutlets. Fed'ka grew such a belly on him, that he made himself a corset and took to wearing it.

Fed'ka was an unscrupulous man: he took money from children he met in the street, he tripped up old men and he terrorized old women by raising his hand to them and, when a frightened old woman shied to one side, Fed'ka would pretend that he had only raised his hand to scratch his head.

It ended when Nikolay went up to Fed'ka, bashed him across the chops and hid under a cupboard.

Fed'ka got Nikolay out with a poker from under the cupboard and ripped open his mouth.

Nikolay ran off with his ripped mouth to the neighbours, but Fed'ka caught up with him and clubbed him with a beermug. Nikolay collapsed and died.

Fed'ka gathered his things and went away from Vladivostok.

(Written in two devices, by 21 November 1937)

A New Talented Writer

Andrey Andreyevich thought up a story like this one.

In an old castle there lived a prince, who was a terrible boozer. But the wife of this prince, on the contrary, didn't even drink tea, she only drank water and milk. While her husband drank vodka and wine, but didn't drink milk.

Though, in fact, his wife, to tell the truth, also drank vodka but kept it quiet. But her husband was quite shameless and didn't keep it quiet.

– I don't drink milk, I drink vodka! – he always said. While his wife, on the quiet, from under her apron, pulled out a jar and – glug! – she was drinking away.

Her husband, the prince, says: – You could have given me some. –

But his wife, the princess, says: – No, there's little enough for me. Shoo!

– As for you, – says the prince – call yourself a lady! – And with these words, wallop, and his wife's on the floor! The wife, her whole kisser smashed in, lies on the floor crying. And the prince wrapped himself in his cloak and went to his quarters in the tower, where his cages stood. He bred fowls there, you see. And so the prince arrived in the tower and there the chickens were squawking, wanting food. One chicken even began to neigh.

– As for you – said the prince – you Chauntecleer! Shut up, before you get your teeth bashed in! – The chicken doesn't understand a word and just carries on neighing. So, in the end then, we've got a chicken making a racket in the tower, and the prince, then, effing and blinding and his wife, then, downstairs lying on the floor – in a word, a complete Sodom.

That's the sort of story Andrey Andreyevich would think up. Even just from this story you can tell that Andrey Andreyevich is a major talent. Andrey Andreyevich is a very clever man. Very clever and very fine!

(1938)

[They Call Me the Capuchin]

They call me the Capuchin. For that I'll tear the ears off whomsoever it may be necessary, but meanwhile I get no peace from the fame of Jean-Jacques Rousseau. Why did he have to know everything? How to swaddle infants and how to give young girls in marriage! I would also like to know everything. In fact I do know everything, except that I am not so sure of my theories. About infants, I certainly know that they should not be swaddled at all – they should be obliterated. For this I would establish a central pit in the city and would throw the infants into it. And so that the stench of decomposition should not come from the pit, it could be flooded every week with quicklime. Into the same pit I would stick all Alsatian dogs. Now, about giving young girls in marriage. That, in my view, is even simpler: I would establish a public hall where, say, once a month all the youth would assemble. All of them between seventeen and thirty-five would have to strip naked and parade up and down the hall. If anyone fancied someone, then that pair would go off into a corner and there examine each other in detail. I forgot to say that they would all have to have a card hanging from the neck with their name, surname and address. Then, a letter could be sent to whomever was to someone's taste, to set up a more intimate acquaintance. Should any old man or woman intervene in these matters, I would propose killing them with an axe and dragging them off to the same place as the infants – to the central pit.

I would have written more on my current theories, but unfortunately I have to go to the shop for tobacco. When walking on the street, I always take with me a thick knotty stick. I take it with me in order to batter any infants who may get under my feet. That must be why they called me the Capuchin. But just you wait, you swine, I'll skin your ears yet!

(1938)

The Artist and the Clock

Serov, an artist, went to the Obvodniy Canal. Why did he go there? To buy some india rubber. What did he want india rubber for? To make himself a rubber band. And what did he want a rubber band for? In order to stretch it. That's what for. And what else? This is what else: the artist Serov had broken his clock. The clock had been going well, but he picked it up and broke it. What else? Nothing else. Nothing, this is it, in a nutshell! Keep your filthy snout out when it's not needed! And may the Lord have mercy on us!

Once there lived an old woman. She lived and loved, until she got burnt up in her stove. Served her right, too! The artist Serov, at least, was of that opinion . . .

Huh! I would write some more, but the ink-pot has suddenly gone and disappeared.

(1938)

[I Had Raised Dust]

I had raised dust. Children were running after me, tearing their clothing. Old men and old women fell from roofs. I whistled, I roared, my teeth chattered and I clattered like an iron bar. Lacerated children raced after me and, falling behind, broke their thin legs in their awful haste. Old men and old women were skipping around me. I rushed on! Filthy, rachitic children, looking like toadstools, got tangled under my feet. Running was hard going. I kept remembering things and once I even almost fell into the soft mush of old men and women floundering on the ground. I jumped, snapped a few heads off toadstools and trod on the belly of a thin old woman, who at this emitted a loud crunch and softly muttered: – They've worn me out. – Not looking back, I ran on further. Now under my feet was a clean and smooth pavement. Occasional streetlamps lit my way. I ran up to the bath-house. The welcoming bath-house flickered in front of me and the cosy but stifling bath-house steam was already in my nostrils, ears and mouth. Without undressing, I ran straight through the changing-room, then past the taps, the tubs and the planks, to the shelf. A hot white cloud surrounds me, I hear a weak but insistent sound. I seem to be lying down.

And at this point, a mighty relaxation stopped my heart.

(1939)

[A Shortish Gent . . .]

A shortish gent with a pebble in his eye went up to the door of a tobacconist's shop and stopped. His black polished shoes gleamed on the stone step leading up to the tobacconist's. The toe-caps of his shoes were directed at the inside of the shop. Two more steps and the gentleman would have disappeared through the door. But for some reason he dilly-dallied, as though purposely to position his head under the brick which was falling from the roof. The gentleman had even taken off his hat, baring his bald skull, and thus the brick struck the gentleman right on his bare head, broke the cranium and embedded itself in his brain. The gentleman didn't fall. No, he merely staggered a bit from the terrible blow, pulled a handkerchief from his pocket, used it to wipe his face, which was all gooey from blood and brains, and, turning towards the crowd, which had instantly gathered around the gentleman, he said: – Don't worry, ladies and gents: I've already had the vaccination. You can see – I've got a protruding pebble in my right eye. That was also once quite an incident. I've already got used to that. Now everything's just fine and dandy!

And with these words the gentleman replaced his hat and went off somewhere into the margins, leaving the troubled crowd in complete bewilderment.

(1939–1940)

Knights

There was a house, full of old women. The old women lounged around the house all day and swatted flies with paper bags. There were in all thirty-six old women in this house. The most vigorous old woman, by surname Yufleva, ordered the other old women about. She would nip any disobedient old woman on the back of the shoulders or trip her up, and she would fall and smash her face. One old woman called Zvyakina, punished by Yufleva, fell so disastrously that she broke both her jaws. The doctor had to be sent for. He arrived, put on his white coat and, having examined Zvyakina, said that she was too old for there being any possibility of counting on her jaws mending. Then the doctor asked to be given a hammer, a chisel, pincers and rope. The old women drifted round the house for ages and, not knowing what pincers and a chisel look like, they brought the doctor everything that seemed to them anything like tools. The doctor cursed for a long time but finally, having received all the objects he had demanded, asked everyone to withdraw. The old women, burning with curiosity, withdrew with great displeasure. When the old women, amid swearing and grumbling, had flocked out of the room, the doctor locked the door behind them and went up to Zvyakina.

– Now then – said the doctor and, having grabbed Zvyakina, tied her tightly with the rope. Then the doctor, paying no attention to the loud cries and wailing of Zvyakina, placed the chisel to her jaw-bone and struck the chisel hard with the hammer. Zvyakina began howling in a hoarse bass. Having shattered Zvyakina's jaw with the chisel, the doctor grabbed the pincers and, having engaged Zvyakina's jaws, tore them out. Zvyakina howled, shouted and wheezed, covered in blood. And the doctor dropped the pincers and Zvyakina's torn out jaw-bones on the floor, took off his white coat, wiped his hands on it and, going over to the door, opened it. The old women tumbled into the room with a scream and stared goggle-eyed, some at Zvyakina, some at the blood-stained bits lying about on the floor. The doctor pushed his way between the old women and went out. The old women rushed over to Zvyakina. Zvyakina faded in volume and, obviously, was in the process of dying. Yufleva stood right there, looking at Zvyakina and nibbling at sunflower seeds. The old woman Byashechina said: – So, Yufleva, even you and I will snuff it some day.

Yufleva kicked at Byashechina, but the latter jumped aside in time.

– Come on girls! – said Byashechina. – Why hang around here? Let's leave Yufleva and Zvyakina to romp around, and we'll go and swat flies.

And the old women moved off out of the room.

Yufleva, continuing to bite into her sunflower seeds, stood in the middle of the room and looked at Zvyakina. Zvyakina had faded away and lay there motionless. Perhaps she had died.

However, with this the author is finishing his narrative, since he cannot find his ink-pot.

(1940)

The Lecture

Pushkov said: — Woman — is the workbench of love.

And he immediately received a clout across the gob.

— What's that for? — asked Pushkov.

But, not getting any answer to his question, he continued: — This is what I think: a woman should be tackled from below. Women really like this and only pretend that they don't like it.

At this point Pushkov was again struck across the gob.

— But what on earth is this, comrades! If that's the way it is, I won't carry on speaking — said Pushkov.

But, after waiting about a quarter of a minute, he continued: — A woman is so built that she is all soft and damp.

At this point Pushkov was again struck across the gob. Pushkov tried to pretend that he hadn't noticed this and went on: — If you just sniff a woman . . .

But at this point Pushkov was so slammed across the gob that he caught hold of his cheek and said: — Comrades, under these conditions it is absolutely impossible to deliver a lecture. If this happens again, I shall discontinue.

Pushkov waited for a quarter of a minute and then continued: — Now, where were we? Ah, yes. That was it. A woman loves to look at herself. She sits down in front of the mirror completely naked . . .

At this word, Pushkov again received a clout across the gob.

— Naked — repeated Pushkov.

Smack! — he was weighed into right across the gob.

— Naked! — yelled Pushkov.

Smack! — he received a clout across the gob.

— Naked! A naked woman! A nude tart! — Pushkov kept yelling.

Smack! Smack! Smack! – Pushkov took it across the gob.

– A nude tart with a ladle in her hands! – yelled Pushkov.

Smack! Smack! – the blows rained down on Pushkov.

– A tart's bum-hole! – yelled Pushkov, dodging the blows. – A nude nun!

But at this point Pushkov was struck with such force that he lost consciousness and crumpled to the floor as though pole-axed.

(1940)

Myshin's Triumph

They said to Myshin: – Hey, Myshin, get up!

Myshin said: – I won't get up – and continued lying on the floor.

Then Kalugin came up to Myshin and said: If you don't get up, Myshin, I will make you get up.

– No – said Myshin, continuing to lie on the floor.

Selizneva went up to Myshin and said: – Myshin, you are for ever sprawling about the floor in the corridor and you interfere with us walking backwards and forwards.

– I have been interfering and I shall keep on interfering – said Myshin.

– Well, you know – said Korshunov, but Kalugin interrupted him and said:

– What's the point of carrying on long conversations about it! Call the militia.

They called for the militia and called out a militiaman.

The militiaman arrived after half an hour with the caretaker.

– What's going on here? – asked the militiaman.

– How do you like this! – said Korshunov, but Kalugin interrupted him and said:

– This is the situation. This citizen lies here on the floor all the time and interferes with us walking along the corridor. We've tried telling him this and that . . .

But at this point Kalugin was interrupted by Selizneva, who said: – We've asked him to go away, but he doesn't go away.

– Yes – said Korshunov.

The militiaman went up to Myshin.

– You, citizen, why are you lying here? – asked the militiaman.

– I'm resting – said Myshin.

– Resting here is not good enough, citizen – said the militiaman. – Where do you live, citizen?

– Here – said Myshin.

– Where's your room? – asked the militiaman.

– He's registered in our flat, but he doesn't have a room – said Kalugin.

– Wait a minute, citizen – said the militiaman – I'll have a word with him now. Citizen, where do you sleep?

– Here – said Myshin.

– Allow me to – said Korshunov, but Kalugin interrupted him and said:

– He doesn't even have a bed and he sprawls right on the bare floor.

– They've been complaining about him for a long time – said the caretaker.

– It's absolutely impossible to walk along the corridor – said Selizneva – I can't keep stepping over a man for ever. And he sticks out his legs on purpose, and he sticks out his hands, and he lies on his back and looks up. I come back tired from work, I need a rest.

– And I can add – said Korshunov, but Kalugin interrupted him and said:

– He lies here at night, as well. Everyone trips over him in the dark. I tore my blanket because of him.

Selizneva said: – He's always got tin-tacks and things falling out of his pocket. It's impossible to walk barefooted down the corridor, or before you know where you are – you put your foot on something.

– They wanted to set him alight with kerosene the other day – said the caretaker.

– We did pour kerosene over him – said Korshunov, but Kalugin interrupted him and said:

– We only poured kerosene over him to scare him, but we weren't going to set light to him.

– Oh no, I wouldn't have a man burned alive in my presence – said Selizneva.

– But why is this citizen lying in the corridor? – the militiaman suddenly asked.

– That's a fine how do you do! – said Korshunov, but Kalugin interrupted him and said:

– Well, because he hasn't got any other living space: here's where I live, in this room, and she's in that one, and that one's his, and so Myshin lives here, in the corridor.

– That's not good enough – said the militiaman. – Everyone should be lying in their own living space.

– But he hasn't got any other living space, except in the corridor – said Kalugin.

– That's just it – said Korshunov.

– And so he goes on lying here – said Selizneva.

– That's not good enough – said the militiaman and went away, together with the caretaker.

Korshunov leaped over to Myshin.

– What about it? – he yelled. – How did you like that, then?

– Wait – said Kalugin. And, going up to Myshin, he said: – Did you hear what the militiaman said? Get up from the floor!

– I won't get up – said Myshin, continuing to lie there on the floor.

– Now he will deliberately and furthermore and for ever keep on lying there – said Selizneva.

– Definitely – said Kalugin with some irritation.

And Korshunov said: – I don't doubt it. *Parfaitement!*

(1940)

The Falling

Two men fell from a roof. They both fell from the roof of a five-storey newly erected building. Seemingly a school. They had moved down the roof in a sitting position to the very edge and at that point started to fall. Their fall was noticed first of all by Ida Markovna. She was standing at her window in the building opposite and was blowing her nose into a tumbler. And suddenly she caught sight of someone starting to fall from the roof of the building opposite. Peering out, Ida Markovna saw what was an entire twosome starting to fall at once. Completely losing her head, Ida Markovna tore off her shift and hurriedly began to rub the misted-over window-pane, the better to make out who was falling from the roof out there. However, twigging that, perhaps, those falling might, from their vantage point, be able to glimpse her naked

– and goodness only knew what they might think of her – Ida Markovna jumped back from the window and hid behind the wicker tripod on which there had at one time stood a pot plant.

At this juncture, those falling from the roof were sighted by another personage who lived in the same building as Ida Markovna, only two floors below. This personage was also called Ida Markovna. She happened at the time to be sitting with her feet up on the window-sill and was sewing a button on her slipper. Looking out of the window, she had caught sight of those falling from the roof. Ida Markovna yelped and, leaping up from the window-sill, hastily began opening the window, so as to get a better view when those falling from the roof should strike the ground. But the window would not open. Ida Markovna remembered that she had nailed the window from beneath and rushed to the stove, in which she kept her tools: four hammers, a chisel and pincers. Grabbing the pincers, Ida Markovna again ran up to the window and pulled out the nail. Now the window was easily flung open. Ida Markovna leaned out of the window and saw those who had fallen from the roof whistling towards the ground.

On the street a smallish crowd had already gathered. Whistles were already blowing and a diminutive militiaman was unhurriedly approaching the location of the anticipated event. A big-nosed caretaker bustled about, shoving people and explaining that those falling from the roof could smite the heads of those gathered below. By this time, both Ida Markovnas – the one in a dress and the other naked – having leaned out of their windows, were squealing and kicking their legs about. And so, finally, arms spread and eyes agape, those who had fallen from the roof struck the ground.

Just as on occasion we, falling from heights we have attained, may strike the dreary cage of our future.

(Written over four days. Finished [7 October] 1940)

[Perechin]

Perechin sat on a drawing pin and, from this moment, his life changed abruptly. From a contemplative, quiet man Perechin turned into a downright scoundrel. He grew himself a moustache and henceforth trimmed it extremely untidily, in such a way that the one side of his moustache was always longer than the other. And so his moustache came to grow somehow askew. It became impossible to look at Perechin. What is more, he would give a repulsive wink of the eye and twitch his cheek. For a certain time Perechin confined himself to petty and reprehensible tricks: he told tales, denounced people, and cheated tram conductors by paying them his fare in the very smallest copper coin and each time two or three kopecks short.

(1940)

The Drawback

Pronin said: – You have very beautiful stockings.

Irina Mazer said: – Do you like my stockings?

Pronin said: – Oh yes. Very much. – And he made a grab at them with his hand.

Irina said: – But why do you like my stockings?

Pronin said: – They are very smooth.

Irina lifted her skirt and said: – And do you see how high they go?

Pronin said: – Oh yes, I do.

Irina said: – But here they come to an end. Up here it's bare leg.

– Oh, and what leg! – said Pronin.

– I've got very thick legs – said Irina. – And I'm very wide in the hips.

– Show me – said Pronin.

– I can't – said Irina. – I've no knickers on.

Pronin got down on his knees in front of her.

Irina said: – What are you kneeling for?

Pronin kissed her on the leg, a little above the stocking top, and said: – That's what for.

Irina said: – Why are you lifting my skirt even higher? I've already told you I've no knickers on.

But Pronin lifted her skirt all the same and said: – Never mind, never mind.

– What do you mean, never mind? – said Irina.

But at this juncture someone was knocking at the door. Irina briskly pulled down her skirt and Pronin got up from the floor and went over to the window.

– Who's there? – asked Irina through the door.

– Open the door – said a sharp voice.

Irina opened the door and into the room came a man in a black coat and high boots. Behind him came a pair of soldiers of the lowest rank, rifles at the ready, and behind them came the caretaker. The lower ranks stood by the door, while the man in the black coat went up to Irina Mazer and said: – Your name?

– Mazer – said Irina.

– Your name? – asked the man in the black coat, turning to Pronin.

Pronin said: – My name is Pronin.

– Do you have a weapon? – asked the man in the black coat.

– No – said Pronin.

– Sit down here – said the man in the black coat, indicating a chair to Pronin.

Pronin sat down.

– And you – said the man in the black coat, turning to Irina, – put your coat on. You'll have to come for a ride with us.

– What for? – asked Irina.

The man in the black coat did not reply.

– I'll need to change – said Irina.

– No – said the man in the black coat.

– But there's something else I need to put on – said Irina.

– No – said the man in the black coat.

Irina put on her fur coat in silence.

– Good bye, then – she said to Pronin.

– Conversations are not allowed – said the man in the black coat.

– Do I come with you as well? – asked Pronin.

– Yes – said the man in the black coat. – Get your coat on.

Pronin stood up, took his coat and hat down from the peg, put them on and said: – Well, I'm ready.

– Let's go – said the man in the black coat.

The lower ranks and the caretaker stamped their feet.

They all went out into the corridor.

The man in the black coat locked the door of Irina's room and sealed it with two brown seals.

– Outside – he said.

And they all went out of the flat, loudly slamming the outside door.

(1940)

Symphony No. 2

Anton Mikhailovich spat, said 'ugh', spat again, again said 'ugh', again spat, again said 'ugh' and walked away. And to hell with him. I'd do better to talk about Il'ya Pavlovich.

Il'ya Pavlovich was born in 1893 in Constantinople.

When he was still a small boy, he was taken to Petersburg and here he went to the German school on Kirochnaya Street. Then he worked in some shop or other, then he did something else and at the beginning of the revolution he emigrated abroad. Well and to hell with him. I'd do better to talk about Anna Ignat'evna.

But to talk about Anna Ignat'evna is not so very simple. In the first place I don't know anything about her and in the second place I have now fallen off my chair and forgotten what I had intended to say. I'd do better to talk about myself.

I am on the tall side, quite intelligent, I'm a flashy dresser with a bit of taste, I don't drink, I don't go to the races, but I do chase the ladies. And the ladies don't avoid me. They even like it when I muck around with them. Serafima Izmailovna has often invited me round and Zinaida Yakovlevna also used to say that she was always pleased to see me. But there did occur between me and Marina Pavlovna an amusing incident which I want to tell you about. It was a completely ordinary incident, but all the same an amusing one for, thanks to me, Marina Pavlovna went absolutely bald, like the palm of your hand. It happened like this: once I arrived at Marina Pavlovna's and bang! – she went bald. And that's all there is to it.

(1941)

Rehabilitation

Without boasting, I can tell you that, when Volodya struck me across the ear and spat in my face, I really got him, so that he won't forget it. It was only after that that I hit him with the primus and it was evening when I hit him with the iron. So he didn't die straight away by any means. This doesn't prove that I cut his leg off as early as the afternoon. He was still alive then. Whereas Andryusha I killed simply from inertia, and I can't hold myself responsible for that. Why did Andryusha and Yelizaveta Antonovna fall into my hands anyway? They had no business springing out from behind the door. I am being accused of bloodthirstiness; they say I drank blood, but that's not true: I licked up the pools of blood and the stains – it is a man's natural urge to wipe out the traces of even the most trivial of crimes. And also I did not rape Yelizaveta Antonovna. In the first place, she was no longer a virgin; and secondly I was having dealings with a corpse, so she has no cause for complaint. What about the fact that she just happened to have to give birth? Well, I did pull out the infant. The fact that he was not long for this world anyway, well that's really not my fault. I didn't tear his head off; it was his thin neck that did that. He was simply not created for this life. It's true that I stomped their dog to a pulp around the floor, but it's really cynical to accuse me of murdering the dog when in the immediate vicinity, it might be said, three human lives had been obliterated. The infant I don't count. Well, all right then, in all this (I can agree with you) it is possible to discern a degree of severity on my part. But to consider it a crime that I squatted down and defecated on my victims – that is really, if you'll excuse me, absurd. Defecation is an urge of nature and consequently can in no sense be criminal. All things considered, I do understand the misgivings of my defence counsel, but all the same I am hoping for a complete acquittal.

([10 July] 1941)

YELIZAVETA BAM:
A DRAMATIC WORK

YELIZAVETA BAM

DRAMATIS PERSONAE
Yelizaveta [Elizabeth] Bam
Pyotr Nikolayevich [First Voice]
Ivan Ivanovich [Second Voice]
Daddy
Mummy
Beggar
various voices, noises, instruments, a choir etc. – offstage, or
from the hall

(*Decor – stage: a shallow, simple room*)

1st bit. Realistic melodrama

YELIZAVETA BAM Now, I'm afraid, the door will open and
they'll come in ... They'll definitely come
in, to catch me and wipe me from the face of
the earth. (*Quietly*) What have I done! What
have I done! If only I knew ... Run away?
(*A footstep*) But run away where? This door
opens on to the staircase, and I'll meet them
on the staircase. Through the window?

155

(*Looks out of the window*) Ooh-er, it's so high! I couldn't jump! So what shall I do? . . . Oh! someone's footsteps! It's them. I'll lock the door and won't open it. Let them knock as long as they like.

Knock at the door, then a VOICE *threateningly*

VOICE	Elizabeth Bam, open up!
	Elizabeth Bam, open up!
DISTANT VOICE	(*Behind stage*) What's she up to in there, won't she open the door?
VOICE BEHIND THE DOOR	She'll open it. Yelizaveta Bam, open up!

Eliz. Bam throws herself onto the bed and covers her ears.
Voices behind the door

FIRST	Elizabeth Bam, I am ordering you to open up immediately!
SECOND	(*Quietly*) You tell her that if she doesn't we'll break the door down. Let me try.
FIRST	(*Loudly*) We'll break the door down if you don't open up right away.
SECOND	(*Quietly*) Perhaps she's not here?
FIRST	(*Quietly*) She's here. Where else would she be? She ran up the staircase. There's only one door here. Where else could she get to? (*Loudly*) Yelizaveta Bam – it's speaking to you I am.

Eliz. Bam raises her head.

For the last time, open the door. (*A pause*) Break it down.

With an alliterative ring, they try to break the door down. Eliz. Bam runs to the middle of the stage, listening.

SECOND   Haven't you got a knife?

A bang at the door. Eliz. Bam listens, her shoulder thrust forward.

FIRST   No, use your shoulder.

SECOND   It won't give. Wait a minute, I'll try again. (*The door creaks, but doesn't break*)

ELIZ. BAM   I won't open the door to you until you tell me what you intend to do with me.

The knocking quietens at ELIZ. BAM's *retort.*

FIRST VOICE   You know yourself what you are in for.

ELIZ. BAM   No, I don't. Are you going to kill me?

FIRST (*Together*)   You are liable to stringent punishment!

SECOND   You won't get away from us, whatever happens!

ELIZ. BAM   Perhaps you would tell me what offence I have committed.

FIRST   You know yourself.

ELIZ. BAM   No, I don't know. (*Stamps her foot*)

FIRST   Excuse us if we don't believe you.

SECOND   You are a criminal.

ELIZ. BAM   Ha, ha ha! And if you kill me, do you think your conscience will be clear? (*Runs across*)

FIRST   We'll take care of it, in due conformity with our conscience.

ELIZ. BAM   In that case then, alas, you can't have any conscience.

2nd bit. *The genre of realistic comedy*

SECOND   What do you mean, no conscience? Pyotr
                Nikolayevich, she says that we have no
                conscience.

ELIZ. BAM   (*Standing, hands on thighs and neck craned
                towards the door*) You, Ivan Ivanovich, have
                no conscience whatsoever. You are just a
                scoundrel.

SECOND   Who's a scoundrel? Me? I am? I am a
                scoundrel?!

FIRST   Now, hang on a minute, Ivan Ivanovich!
                Elizabeth Bam, I order you to ...

SECOND   No, Pyotr Nikolayevich, would you say that
                I am the scoundrel here?

FIRST   Hang on a minute before you take
                umbrage! Yelizaveta Bam, I'm ord ...

SECOND   No, just a mo, Pyotr Nikolayevich. Are you
                going to tell me that I'm a scoundrel?

FIRST   Leave it off, will you!

SECOND   You mean, you do think I'm a scoundrel?

FIRST   Yes, a scoundrel!!!

SECOND   So that's it, you think I'm a scoundrel! Is
                that what you said?

ELIZ. BAM *runs about the stage.*

FIRST   You'd better just bugger off then, you dun-
                derhead! And you're supposed to be con-
                ducting a responsible inquiry. The first
                word that's said to you and you go up the
                wall. What does that make you? Just an
                idiot!

SECOND	And you're a charlatan!
FIRST	Just bugger off!
ELIZ. BAM	Ivan Ivanovich is a scoundrel!
SECOND	I won't forgive you for this!
FIRST	I'll throw you down the staircase in a minute!

ELIZ. BAM *opens the door.* IVAN IVANOVICH *stands there on crutches, and* PYOTR NIKOLAYEVICH *is sitting on a chair with a bandaged cheek.*

IVAN IVANOVICH	Just you try it!
PYOTR NIKO-LAYEVICH	I will, I will, I will, I will!
ELIZ. BAM	No chance!
PYOTR NIK.	I've no chance, you mean?
ELIZ. BAM *(together)*	Yes
IVAN IV.	You! You! You mean him, don't you? (IVAN IV. *points to* PYOTR NIK.
ELIZ. BAM	Him!
PYOTR NIK.	Elizabeth Bam, how dare you speak like that!
ELIZ. BAM	Why shouldn't I?
PYOTR NIK.	Because you have lost all right of reply. You have committed a vile crime. It's not for you to be impertinent to me. You are a criminal!
ELIZ. BAM	Why?
PYOTR NIK.	What do you mean, why?
ELIZ. BAM	Why am I a criminal?
PYOTR NIK.	Because you have lost all right of reply.
IVAN IV.	Lost all right of reply.
ELIZ. BAM	I haven't lost any such thing. You can check by the clock.

The stage backcloth moves back, letting IVAN IV. *and* PYOTR NIK. *through the door.*

3rd bit. Absurdly comic-naive

PYOTR NIK.	It won't come to that. I have placed a guard on the door, and at the slightest push Ivan Ivanovich will hiccup an aside.
ELIZ. BAM	A demonstration, please, a demonstration.
PYOTR NIK	Just look, then. I suggest you avert your eyes. (PYOTR NIK. *comes to the proscenium,* IVAN IV. *follows him*) One, two, three. (*Touches the pedestal,* IVAN IV. *hiccups loudly.* PYOTR NIK. *turns the pedestal over*)
ELIZ. BAM	And again, please. (*They repeat it.* PYOTR NIK. *again touches the pedestal and* IVAN IV. *again hiccups.*) How do you do it?
PYOTR NIK.	It's very simple. Ivan Ivanovich, demonstrate.
IVAN IV.	With pleasure. (*Gets down on his hands and knees and kicks one leg in the air*)
ELIZ. BAM	Oh, it's charming, it's so good (*Shouts*) Mum! Come here! The conjurers have arrived! My mother will be here in just a moment ... You must meet her, Pyotr Nikolayevich! Ivan Ivanovich! Are you going to show us something?
IVAN IV.	With pleasure.
PYOTR NIK.	Allez-oop!

IVAN IV. *tries to stand on his head, but topples.*

PYOTR NIK.	He'll do it now, right away.

On stage come DADDY *and* MUMMY, *who sit down and watch.*

IVAN IV.	(*Sitting on the floor*) There's nothing to lean on here.
ELIZ. BAM	(*Flirtingly*): Would you like a towel perhaps?
IVAN IV.	What for?
ELIZ. BAM	Oh, not for anything in particular. Tee-hee-hee.
IVAN IV.	I say, you do have an extraordinarily pleasant appearance.
ELIZ. BAM	Oh really? Why is that?
IVAN IV.	Ee-ee-ee-ee-, because you're a forget-me-not (*Loudly hiccups*).
ELIZ. BAM	I'm a forget-me-not? Really? And you are a tulip (*In a nasal tone*).
IVAN IV.	What?
ELIZ. BAM	A tulip.
IVAN IV.	(*In some perplexity*) Thank you very much, I'm sure.
ELIZ. BAM	(*Nasally*): Allow me to pluck you.
DADDY	(*In a bass voice*): Elizabeth, don't be silly.
ELIZ. BAM	(*To father*): Daddy, I'll stop right away. (*Squatting, her hands resting on her knees; to* IVAN IV. *nasally*) Get down on your hands and knees.

PYOTR NIK. *goes over to* DADDY *and* MUMMY. MUMMY, *displeased at something, moves down stage.*

IVAN IV.	If you will allow me, Elizabeth Cockroach, I had better be getting home. My wife's waiting for me at home. She has lots of children, Elizabeth Cockroach. Forgive me for boring

you so. Don't forget me. I'm the sort of
person everyone sends on errands. Why,
one wonders? Am I a thief, or something?
Certainly not! Yelizaveta Edwardovna, I'm
an honest man. I have a wife at home. My
wife has children, lots of them. Nice children. They keep holding a matchbox in their
teeth, every one of them. Please forgive me.
I'm going home, Yelizaveta Mikhaylovna.

IVAN IV. *puts on his fur coat and goes out.* ELIZ. BAM *ties a rope to*
MUMMY's *leg — the other end she ties to a chair. They all remain
silent.*

MUMMY   (*sings to music*) Morning has broken
                 Like the first morning.
                 Blackbird has spoken
                 Like the first bird.

MUMMY *finishes her song and goes back to her place, dragging the
chair behind her.*

PYOTR NIK.   Well, here we are!
DADDY   Thank God for that! (*They leave the stage*)

4th bit. Realistic. Everyday comic genre.

ELIZ. BAM   And you, Mummy, are you really not going
                 out?
MUMMY   Do you feel like it?
ELIZ. BAM   Awfully.
MUMMY   No, I'm not going.
ELIZ. BAM   Let's go, come on.

162

MUMMY   Well, let's go then, let's go.

They go out. The stage is empty.

5th bit. Rhythmic (RADIX), author's rhythm.

IVAN IV. and   (*Running in*) Oh where, where, where
PYOTR NIK.   is Yelizaveta Bam,
Yelizaveta Bam.
Yelizaveta Bam.

PYOTR NIK.   Here, here, here.

IVAN IV.   There, there, there.

PYOTR NIK.   (*Syncopated verse*) Oh, Ivan Ivanovich, what
is our result?

IVAN IV.   Why, Pyotr Nikolayevich, we're under lock
and key.

PYOTR NIK.   Well, that is just outrageous! It's not me that
you should clout!

IVAN IV.   Here's a pound for you, and it's five minus
five for me!

PYOTR NIK.   (*melodiously*): Where, oh where is Elizabeth
Bam?

IVAN IV.   Why do you want her, you big ham?

PYOTR NIK.   Oh, to kill her!

IVAN IV.   Well, now, Elizabeth Bam
Is sitting there: if you want her, scram!

PYOTR NIK.   We'd better start running then, feller!

*Both start running on the spot. A log is brought on frontstage and
while* PYOTR NIK. *and* IVAN IV. *are running, the log is being sawn.*

BOTH   Hop, hop
move your stumps

the sun is setting
over the humps
big clouds of rosy hue
puff, puff
of chuff-chuff
toowit-towoo
the owl does coo
    that log! –
    it's all sawn through.

6th bit. Everyday RADIX

A flap is moved back and behind the flap sits ELIZ. BAM.

ELIZ. BAM	Are you looking for me?
PYOTR NIK.	Yes, you! Van'ka, she's here!
IVAN IV.	Where, where, where?
PYOTR NIK.	'ere, under the thingamy!

On stage comes a BEGGAR.

IVAN IV.	Pull her out here!
PYOTR NIK.	She won't come!
BEGGAR	(*to* ELIZ. BAM) Comrade, help me out.
IVAN IV.	(*Stammering*) Next time I'll have more experience. I've just been watching points.
ELIZ. BAM	(*to* BEGGAR) I have nothing.
BEGGAR	Just a kopeck.
ELIZ. BAM	Ask that bloke over there (*pointing at* PYOTR NIK.).

A table is wheeled out on stage; ELIZ. BAM *brings a chair over to it and sits down.*

PYOTR NIK.	(*To* IVAN IV., *stammering*) You just look what you are doing!
IVAN IV.	(*Stammering*) I'm digging up roots.
BEGGAR	Help me out, comrades.
PYOTR NIK.	(*to* BEGGAR) Come on. Get in there.
IVAN IV.	Hold on to the pebbles with your hands.

The BEGGAR *climbs under the flap.*

PYOTR NIK.	That's not bad, he can do it.
ELIZ. BAM	You sit down, too. Why don't you?

Pause

IVAN IV.	Thank you.
PYOTR NIK.	Let's sit down. (*They sit down; silence; they eat soup.*)
ELIZ. BAM	My husband is late, it seems. Where's he got to now?
PYOTR NIK.	He'll come (*Jumps up and runs around the stage*). Mob-mob! Chur-choora!
IVAN IV.	Ha, ha, ha (*runs after* PYOTR NIK.). Where's the 'den'?
ELIZ. BAM	Here, behind this line.

DADDY *comes on stage with a feather in his hand.*

PYOTR NIK.	(*taps* IVAN IV.) You're 'it'.
ELIZ. BAM	Ivan Ivanych, run over here!
IVAN IV.	Ha, ha, ha, I've no legs!
PYOTR NIK.	Go on, like that, on all fours!
DADDY	Concerning whom it was written.
ELIZ. BAM	Who's 'it'?

IVAN IV.	I am, hah, ha, ha, ha, the one in the trousers!
PYOTR NIK. &	
ELIZ. BAM	Ha, ha, ha, ha . . .!
DADDY	Copernicus was a very great scientist.
IVAN IV.	(*Falling to the floor*) I've got hair on my head!
PYOTR NIK. &	
ELIZ. BAM	Ha, ha, ha, ha, hahahaha!
IVAN IV.	I'm completely lying down on the floor!

On stage comes MUMMY.

PYOTR NIK. &	
ELIZ. BAM	Ha, ha, ha, ha, ha!
ELIZ. BAM	Oh, oh, it's too much!
DADDY	When you're buying a bird, make sure it hasn't got teeth. If it's got teeth, it isn't a bird.

7th bit. Solemn melodrama, with undertones of RADIX

PYOTR NIK.	(*Raising his hand*) I must ask you to listen properly to my words. I want to prove to you that every misfortune comes unexpectedly. When I was still a very young man I lived in a small house with a squeaking door. I lived alone in that house. Apart from me there were only mice and cockroaches. You get cockroaches everywhere; when night came on I would lock the door and put out the lamp. I used to sleep, and would be afraid of nothing more.
VOICE OFF	Nothing!
MUMMY	Nothing!

166

(Pipe sounds offstage: three notes) ♩ ♪ ♩

IVAN IV.   Nothing!

(Piano is played: three notes) ♩ ♪ ♩

PYOTR NIK.   Nothing more!

A pause

> I had nothing to be afraid of. Really. Robbers could have come and gone through the whole house. What would they have found? Nothing.

(Pipe sounds off: three notes) ♩ ♪ ♩

Pause

PYOTR NIK.   And who else could get to me at night? Nobody else? At all?
VOICE OFF   Well, was there nobody else?
PYOTR NIK.   At all? But on one occasion, I'm just waking up ...

PYOTR NIK. *and* IVAN IV. *merge together.*

IVAN IV.   ... and I see the door, open, and in the doorway stands some woman or other. I look her right in the eyes. She just stands there. It was light enough. It must have been getting on towards morning. Anyway, I saw her face quite clearly. And this is who

	it was (*points at* ELIZ. BAM). At that time she looked like ...
EVERYONE	Like me!
IVAN IV.	... I speak, therefore I am.
ELIZ. BAM	What are you saying!
IVAN IV.	I speak, therefore I am. It had to be done now. She's listening to me.

Everyone, apart from ELIZ. BAM *and* IVAN IV., *leaves the stage.*

	I asked her what she had done it with. She says they were fighting with spadroons. It was a fair fight, but she's not to blame for killing him. Listen to me, why did you kill Pyotr Nikolayevich?
ELIZ. BAM	Hurray, I didn't kill anyone!
IVAN IV.	To cut him down, just like that! The treachery in that! Hurray! you did it, but why?

8th bit. A displacement of heights

ELIZ. BAM	(*Exits to the side, from where*) Ooh, ooh, ooh-oo-oo.
IVAN IV.	She-wolf.
ELIZ. BAM	Ooh-oo-oo-oo.
IVAN IV.	She-ee-ee-wolf.
ELIZ. BAM	(*Shaking*) Oo-oo-oo-prunes.
IVAN IV.	Your gr-r-r-eat grandmother. (*Lowers his arm*)
ELIZ. BAM	Triumph!
IVAN IV.	You're destroyed for ever. (*Lowers his finger*)
ELIZ. BAM	A black horse, and on the horse a soldier!
IVAN IV.	(*Strikes a match*) My darling Yelizaveta! (IVAN

	IV's *hands shake*)
ELIZ. BAM	My shoulders, like rising suns! (*climbs on chair*)
IVAN IV.	(*Squatting*) My legs, like cucumbers!
ELIZ. BAM	(*Climbing higher*) Hurray! I haven't said a thing!
IVAN IV.	(*Lying down on the floor*) No, no, not a thing, not a thing, gug-ga, psh-psh.
ELIZ. BAM	(*Raising her arm*) Koo-nee-ma-ga-nee-lee-va-nee-ba-ooh, ooh!
IVAN IV.	(*Lying on the floor*) Pussy-cat, pussy-cat taking the milk to task on the cushion she jumped on the stove she jumped jump, jump skip, skip
ELIZ. BAM	(*Shouts*) Gee, a gate! A shirt! a rope!
IVAN IV.	(*Getting up*) Two carpenters come running up and ask: what's up?
ELIZ. BAM	Rissoles! Varvara Semyonna!
IVAN IV.	A dancer on the wi-ire!
ELIZ. BAM	(*Springing up from chair*) I'm all a-glitter!
IVAN IV.	(*Runs to back of room*) The cubic capacity of this room has not been fully calculated by us.

The scenery revolves from living room to countryside. The coulisses give way to DADDY *and* MUMMY.

ELIZ. BAM	(*Runs to the other end of the stage*) It's a family affair!

9th bit. Pastoral bit

IVAN IV.	(*Jumping onto chair*) The prosperity of the Pennsylvanian shepherd and shep-uh-uh!
ELIZ. BAM	(*Jumping onto other chair*) Ivan Iva-ah!
DADDY	(*Showing a box*) A box made of woo-oo-ooh!
IVAN IV.	(*From the chair*) So lo-o-ong!
DADDY	Here, have a lo-oo-oo!
MUMMY	Coo-ee-ee-ee!
ELIZ. BAM	I've found a brown-cap mush-er-roo-oo-ooh!
IVAN IV.	Let's go down to the lake!
DADDY	Coo-ee-ee-ee!
ELIZ. BAM	Coo-ee-ee-ee!
IVAN IV.	I met Nicky yesterday!
MUMMY	Really-ee-ee-ee!
IVAN IV.	Yes, I did. I met him, I met him. I saw Nicky walking along, carrying some apples. You bought them, did you, I asked? Yes, he said, I bought them. Then he just walked on.
DADDY	You don't say-ay-ay!
IVAN IV.	So yes, I asked him: what, did you buy those apples, then, or steal them? And he said: why should I steal them? I bought them. And he just walked off on his way.
MUMMY	Where did he walk off to?
IVAN IV.	I don't know. He didn't steal them, didn't buy them. Just walked on.

10th bit. Monologue aside, double-intentioned bit

DADDY	With this not particularly amiable salutation, her sister conducted her to a more open spot, where stacked in a pile were golden tables and armchairs and a comple-

ment of about fifteen young maidens, babbling gaily amongst themselves and sitting wherever they could. All these maidens were badly in need of a hot smoothing-iron and all were distinguished by a strange manner of rolling their eyes, not for an instant ceasing to babble.

A maid comes in, carrying a table-cloth and a basket of provisions.

11th bit. Speech

IVAN IV.	My friends, we are all gathered. Hooray!
ELIZ. BAM	Hooray!
MUMMY & DADDY	Hooray!
IVAN IV.	(*Shaking and striking a match*) I want you to know that since I was born thirty-eight years have passed.
MUMMY & DADDY	Hooray!
IVAN IV.	Comrades. I have a home. My wife is waiting at home. She has lots of kids. I've counted – there are ten of them.
MUMMY	(*Straight out, on the spot*) Darya, Marya, Fyodor, Pelageya, Nina, Alexander and four others.
DADDY	Are they all boys?

12th bit. The Chinar-ish bit.

ELIZ. BAM	(*Running round the stage*) I've broken away from everywhere! Broken away and started to run! Broken away and, so, run!

MUMMY	(*Running after* ELIZ. BAM) Sup some soup?
DADDY	Sup some meat? (*Running*)
MUMMY	Sup some flour?

Entracte-cataract

IVAN IV.	Sup some swede?
ELIZ. BAM	Sup some mutton?
DADDY	Sup some rissoles?
MUMMY	Oh, my legs are getting tired!
IVAN IV.	Oh, my arms are getting tired!
ELIZ. BAM	Oh, my scissors are getting tired!
DADDY	Oh, my springs are getting tired!

Behind stage a choir sings to the tune of the overture.

MUMMY	The door's open onto the balcony!
IVAN IV.	I'd like to jump up to the third floor!
ELIZ. BAM	Broken away and started to run!
	Broken away and, so, run!

Music strikes up.

DADDY	Help, my right hand and my nose are the same as my left hand and ear!

All, one after the other, run from the stage.

Choir (to the music of the tune of the overture).
Fare thee well, then.

♫ ♩ ♩
♫ ♩ ♩

Upstairs, they say, is a pine,

and all round, they say, it's dark,
on the pine, they say, is a bed,
and in the bed lies a spouse.
Fare thee well, then.

♫ ♩ ♪
♫ ♩ ♪

Once we ran to
♩ ♪ ♩ an endless house.
And out of the window upstairs there looks
through his glasses a young old man.

Fare thee well, then.

♫ ♩ ♪
♫ ♩ ♪

There then opened the gates,
and there showed themselves

Overture: the lights dim.

13th bit. RADIX

Only PYOTR NIK. *is illuminated.*

IVAN IV.	Now you are broken your chair is broken.
VIOLIN	Pa pa pée pa pa pa pée pa
PYOTR NIK.	Rise like Berlin put on your pelerine.
VIOLIN	pa pa pée pa pa pa pée pa
PYOTR NIK.	Eight minutes fly past unnoticed.
VIOLIN	pa pa pée pa pa

	pa pa pée
PYOTR NIK.	You are made to see
	you arouse the laboureres
	the platoon or the compan-ee
	to carry the machine gun.
DRUM	I--I- ♩ ♫ ♩ ♪
	I--I- ♩ ♫ ♩ ♪
	I--I--I-I ♩ ♫ ♩ ♫ ♩ ♩ ♩
PYOTR NIK.	The tatters, they flew
	week after week.
SIREN & DRUM	Vee-a-a-boom, boom
	Vee-a-a-boom.

The light gradually becomes brighter.

PYOTR NIK.	The droopish bridge didn't notice
	the captain-like shuntish noise.
SIREN	vée-a, vée-a, vée-a, vée-a
PYOTR NIK.	Help me now, please help me
	I've salad and water hanging over me.

Full light.

VIOLIN	pa pa pée pa
	pa pa pée pa

The coulisse gives way to IVAN IV.

14th bit. Classical inspiration

IVAN IV.	Tell me, Pyotr Nikolayevich,
	Have you been there, on yonder hill?
PYOTR NIK.	I'm just back from there.

It's wonderful there.

(Declamation)

Flowers are growing. The trees are rustling.
There stands a poor hut – a small wooden
house,
in the hut a low light burns,
over the light swarm thunderflies,
at windows knock the gnats of the night.
Now and then who flutters in and out under
the roof,
but that old brigand, the nightjar.
The dog agitates the air with its chain
and barks all before it into the void,
while in reply unprepossessing dragon-flies
murmur their spells in every key.

IVAN IV.

And in this small house, all of wood
   which we call our poor hut,
in which a low light shines and shifts,
who, pray, in this small house resides?

PYOTR NIK.

No one resides therein
and the door doesn't open,
therein only mice rub flour between their
palms,
therein only the lamp shines as rosemary
the livelong day sits the anchorite cockroach
on the stove.

IVAN IV.   But who then lights the lamp?
PYOTR NIK.   No one, it burns by itself.
IVAN IV.   But that surely cannot be!
PYOTR NIK.   Empty, stupid words!
There is an infinite movement,
the breathing of the lighter elements,
planetary motion, the earth's rotation,

the crazed alternation of day and night,
the combination of remote nature,
the anger and strength of untamed beasts
and the subjugation by man
of the laws of light and wave.

IVAN IV.   (*lighting a match*): Now I realize, realize,
realize.
I give my thanks and squat
and as always take an interest –
What time is it? Tell me.

PYOTR NIK.   Four. Oh, it's time for dinner!
Ivan Ivanovich, let's go,
but remember that tomorrow night
Yelizaveta Bam will die.

DADDY   (*entering*): Which is Yelizaveta Bam,
who is daughter to me,
whom you want
on the very next night
to kill and string up on that pine,
who is so slender,
so all the beasts around should know
and the entire country?
But I am ordering you
by the might of my arm
to forget Elizabeth Bam,
all laws notwithstanding.

PYOTR NIK.   Just try to stop us,
I'll crush you in an instant,
and then with gilded lashes
I'll break all your joints.
You'll be slit up, puffed up
and floated downwind like a fowl.

IVAN IV.   He knows what's what,

he's my guv'nor and my friend,
with a single movement of the wing
he moves the seas,
with a single swing of his axe
he cuts down forest and mountains –
with just his breath
he is ubiquitously elusive.

DADDY   Let us join battle, sorcerer,
you by word and I by arm,
a minute will pass, an hour will pass,
and yet another more.
Perished be you, perished be me,
quiet let it be 'til – wham!
may then she rejoice, daughter mine,
Yelizaveta Bam.

15th bit. Balladic inspiration

BATTLE OF THE TWO HEROES

Two chairs are brought on stage.

IVAN IV.   The battle of the two heroes!
Text – by Immanuel Krasdeiteirich.
Music – by Veliopag, the Netherlandish
shepherd.
Choreography – by an unknown wayfarer.
The bell will announce the start.

Voices from various parts of the hall

The battle of the two heroes!
Text – by Immanuel Krasdeiteirich!

Music – by Veliopag, the Netherlandish shepherd!
Choreography – by an unknown wayfarer!
The bell will announce the start!
The battle of the two heroes!
(etc.)

BELL Boom, boom, boom, boom, boom.

PYOTR NIK. Kurybéer daramóur
dín-dee-ree
slakatéer paka-rádagou
da kée chéerie kíri-kíri
zan-dudéela khaba-cooler
 hey-ell
khánchoo aná coodie
stóom chi na lákoodie
para voo-ee na lée tenner
 hey-ell
chápoo áchapáli
chapátali már
nabalóchéená
(*Raises his arm*) hey-ell

DADDY Let it fly off to the sun,
that wingèd parrot,
let it fade, the golden
widened day, let it.
Let there through the forest peal
the beats of hoof and hunk,
and with a squeal comes from the wheel
that fundamental trunk.
While the knight at table sits
touching his pointed ends
he'll raise his goblet up and then
o'er goblet he will cry:

I lift this cup
to my rapturous lips,
I toast the very best of all,
to Yelizaveta Bam!
Whose very hands, so spick and span
caressed my robes and furs . . .
Live, Elizabeth Bam, live on,
a hundred thousand years!

PYOTR NIK.   Well, sir, let's begin.
I beg you to follow closely
the wavering of our sabres —
which one whither throws its point
and which takes where its direction. (*Strikes*)

IVAN IV.   Thus I record a thrust on the left!

DADDY   (*Thrusting*) I cut to the side, I cut to the
right, save himself who may!
The oak grove rustles with all its might,
grow, gardens, while ye may.

PYOTR NIK.   Spend less time looking around
and watch rather the movement
of the iron centres and the curdling
of deathly powers.

DADDY *raises his rapier and waves it in declamatory time.*

DADDY   Praise be to iron — carborundum!
It holds pavements together
and, shining by electricity,
tears asunder the enemy!
Praise be to iron! Our battle song!
It alarms the brigand,
bears the infant into youth,
tears asunder the enemy!

Oh battle song! Glory to the feathers!
Through the air they fly,
they fill in the eyes of the faithless,
tear asunder the enemy!
Oh glory to the feathers! Wisdom to the
stone.
It lies neath the portentous pine,
from under it water runs
to meet the dead enemy.

PYOTR NIK. *falls.*

PYOTR NIK.   I've fallen, stricken, to the earth
farewell, Yelizaveta Bam,
come down to my place on the hill,
and fall back with a slam.
And then will run all over you
and up and down your arms,
the mice so wild and after that
the anchorite cockroach – wham!

A bell rings.

You hear now how the bell tolls
on the rooftop, bim and bang.
Forgive me and excuse me please,
Yelizaveta Bam.

IVAN IV.   The battle of the two heroes is over.

PYOTR NIK. *is carried out.*

16th bit. Chimes

ELIZ. BAM	(*Entering*) Ah, Daddy, here you are. I am glad. I've just been to the shop, I've just been buying sweets, I wanted there to be cake for tea.
DADDY	(*Opening the gate*) Phoo, I'm just about worn out.
ELIZ. BAM	But what have you been doing?
DADDY	I've been, er, cutting the wood and I'm totally worn out.
ELIZ. BAM	Ivan Ivanovich, go down to the bar-room and bring us a bottle of beer and some peas.
IVAN IV.	Aha! peas and a half bottle of beer, go down to the bar, and from there, back here.
ELIZ. BAM	Not half a bottle, a bottle of beer, and don't go to the bar, go for the peas!
IVAN IV.	Right away, I'll hide my fur coat in the bar-room and I'll put a half pea-pod on my head.
ELIZ. BAM	Oh no, don't do that, just hurry up, or my Dad will have dropped from cutting wood.
DADDY	Oh women! They have little conception, and in their conceptions they have a vacuum.

17th bit. Physiological inspiration

MUMMY	(*Entering*) Comrades. This Jezebel done my son in.

Two heads poke out from the wings.

HEADS	Who did? Who did?

181

MUMMY	This one here, with her very lips!
ELIZ. BAM	Mummy, Mummy, what are you saying?

IVAN IV. *strikes a match.*

MUMMY	All because of you his life ended as a dead loss.
ELIZ. BAM	Just tell me, who are you talking about?
MUMMY	(*Stone faced*) Eek! Eek! Ee-eek!
ELIZ. BAM	She's gone mad!

DADDY *gets a handkerchief and dances on the spot.*

MUMMY	I'm a cuttle-fish.

The decor begins to turn from countryside into a room. The wings absorb MUMMY *and* DADDY.

ELIZ. BAM	They'll be here in a moment. What have I done!
MUMMY	$3 \times 27 = 81$

18th bit. Realistic dry-official

Scene is as at the beginning.

ELIZ. BAM   They'll definitely come, to catch me and wipe me from the face of the earth. Run away. I should run away. But run away where? This door leads to the staircase, and I'll meet them on the staircase. Through the window? (*Looks out of the window*) Oh-oh, I couldn't jump. It's very high. So what shall I do? Oh! someone's footsteps. It's them. I'll lock the door and won't open it. Let them knock as long as they like. (*Locks the door*)

Knock, then Voice   Elizabeth Bam, in the name of the law, I order you to open this door.

Silence

FIRST VOICE   I order you to open this door!

Silence

SECOND VOICE   (*Quietly*) Let's break down the door.

FIRST VOICE   Elizabeth Bam, open up, otherwise we'll break in ourselves!

ELIZ. BAM   What do you intend to do with me?

FIRST VOICE   You are liable to stringent punishment.

ELIZ. BAM   For what? Why don't you want to tell me what I have done?

FIRST VOICE   You are accused of the murder of Pyotr Nikolayevich Krupernák.

SECOND VOICE   And for that you will answer.

ELIZ. BAM   But I haven't killed anyone!

FIRST VOICE   That the court will decide.

ELIZ. BAM *opens the door.* PYOTR NIK. *and* IVAN IV. *enter dressed as firemen.*

ELIZ. BAM   I am in your power.

PYOTR NIK.   You are arrested, in the name of the law.

IVAN IV.   (*Lighting a match*) Follow us.

19th bit. Operatic ending

ELIZ. BAM	(*Shouts*) Truss me up! Pull me by my locks! Thread me through the trough! I haven't killed anyone! I couldn't kill anyone!

Movement of the coulisses [flap], objects, backcloth and people.

PYOTR NIK.	Elizabeth Bam, calm down!
IVAN IV.	Look into the distance in front of you. (*Loudly hiccups*)
ELIZ. BAM	And in the little house on the hill a light is already burning. The mice are twitching their whiskers, twitching them. And on the stove sits Cockroach Cockroachovich, in his shirt with the reddish collar and an axe in his hands.
PYOTR NIK.	Yelizaveta Bam. Having stretched your arms and extinguished your fixed stare, start walking after me, preserving the equilibrium of your joints and the celebration of your sinews. Follow me.

Exeunt slowly. Darkness.
(*Curtain*)

Written 12 to 24 December, 1927

NON-FICTIONAL AND ASSORTED WRITINGS

Theoretical Pieces
Letters
Autobiographical Writings
Erotica

THEORETICAL PIECES

On the Circle

1. Do not take offence at the following argument. For there is nothing offensive in it, unless one does not consider that the circle may be spoken of in a geometrical sense. If I say that the circle describes four identical radii, and you say: not four, but one, then we have a right to ask one another: why? But I don't want to talk about that kind of description of the circle, but of the perfect description of a circle.

2. The circle is the most perfect flat figure. I am not going to say why in particular that is so. But this fact arises of itself in our consciousness in any consideration of flat figures.

3. Nature is so created that the less noticeable the laws of formation, the more perfect the thing.

4. Nature is also so created that the more impenetrable a thing, the more perfect it is.

5. On perfection, I would say the following: perfection in things is a perfect thing. It is always possible to study a perfect thing or, in other words, in a perfect thing there is always something not studied. If a thing should prove to have been completely studied, then it would cease to be perfect, for only that which is incomplete is perfect – that is to say the infinite.

6. A point is infinitely small and thereby attains perfection,

but at the same time it remains inconceivable. Even the smallest conceivable point would not be perfect.

7. A straight line is perfect, for there is no reason for it not to be infinitely long on both sides, to have neither end nor beginning, and thereby be inconceivable. But by putting pressure on it and limiting it on both sides, we render it conceivable, but at the same time imperfect.

If you believe this, then think on.

(10 July 1931)

8. A straight line, broken at one point, forms an angle. But a straight line which is broken simultaneously at all its points is called a curve. A curve does not have to be of necessity infinitely long. It may be such that we can grasp it freely at a glance and yet at the same time remain inconceivable and infinite. I am talking about a closed curve, in which the beginning and the end are concealed. And the most regular, inconceivable, infinite and ideal curve will be a circle.

(17 July 1931)

On Laughter

1. *Advice to humorous performers*

I have noticed that it is very important to determine the point at which laughter can be induced. If you want the auditorium to laugh, come out on to the stage and stand there in silence until someone bursts out laughing. Then wait a little bit longer until someone else starts laughing, and in such a way that everyone can hear. However, this laughter must be genuine and claqueurs, in such an instance, should not be used. When all this has taken place, then the point at which laughter can be induced has been reached. After this you may proceed to your programme of humour and, rest assured, success is guaranteed.

2. There are several sorts of laughter. There is the average sort of laughter, when the whole hall laughs, but not at full volume. There is the strong sort of laughter, when just one part of the hall or another laughs, but at full volume, and the other part of the hall remains silent as, in this case, the laughter doesn't get to it at all. The former sort of laughter requires vaudeville delivery from a vaudeville actor, but the latter sort is better. The morons don't have to laugh.

(1933)

On Time, Space and Existence

1. A world which is not can not be called existing, because it is not.
2. A world consisting of something unified, homogeneous and continuous can not be called existing, because in such a world there are no parts and, once there are no parts, there is no whole.
3. An existing world must be heterogeneous and have parts.
4. Every two parts are different, because one part will always be *this* one and the other *that* one.

5. If only *this* one exists, then *that* one cannot exist, because, as we have said, only *this* exists. But such a *this* cannot exist, because if *this* exists it must be heterogeneous and have parts. And if it has parts that means it consists of *this* and *that*.

6. If *this* and *that* exist, this means that *not this* and *not that* exist, because if *not this* and *not that* did not exist, then *this* and *that* would be unified, homogeneous and continuous and consequently would also not exist.

7. We shall call the first part *this* and the second part *that* and the transition from one to the other we shall call *neither this nor that*.

8. We shall call *neither this nor that* 'the impediment'.

9. Thus: the basis of existence comprises three elements: *this, the impediment* and *that*.

10. We shall express non-existence as zero or a unity. Therefore we shall have to express existence by the number three.

11. Thus: dividing a unitary void into two parts, we get the trinity of existence.

12. Or: a unitary void, experiencing a certain impediment, splits into parts, which make up the trinity of existence.

13. The impediment is that creator which creates 'something' out of 'nothing'.

14. If *this* one, on its own, is 'nothing' or a non-existent 'something', then the 'impediment' is also 'nothing' or a non-existent 'something'.

15. By this reckoning there must be two 'nothings' or non-existent 'somethings'.

16. If there are two 'nothings' or non-existent 'somethings', then one of them is the 'impediment' to the other, breaking it down into parts and becoming itself a part of the other.

17. In the same way the other, being the impediment to the first, splits it into parts and itself becomes a part of the first.

18. In this way are created, of their own accord, non-existent parts.

19. Three, of their own accord, non-existent parts create the three basic elements of existence.

20. The three, of their own accord, non-existent basic elements of existence, all three together, make up a certain existence.

21. If one of the three basic elements of existence should disappear, then the whole would disappear. So: should the 'impediment' disappear, then *this* one and *that* one would become unitary and continuous and would cease to exist.

22. The existence of our universe generates three 'nothings' or separately, on their own account, three non-existent 'somethings': space, time and something else which is neither time nor space.

23. Time, of its essence, is unitary, homogeneous and continuous and thereby does not exist.

24. Space, of its essence, is unitary, homogeneous and continuous and thereby does not exist.

25. But as soon as space and time enter into a certain mutual relationship they become the impediment, the one of the other, and begin to exist.

26. As they begin to exist, space and time become mutually parts, one of the other.

27. Time, experiencing the impediment of space, breaks down into parts, generating the trinity of existence.

28. A split down and existing, consists of the three basic elements of existence: the past, the present and the future.

29. The past, the present and the future, as basic elements of existence, always stood in inevitable dependence, each on the other. There cannot be a past without a present and a future, or a present without a past and a future, or a future without a past and a present.

30. Examining these three elements separately, we see that there is no past because it has already gone, and there is no future because it has not yet come. That means that there remains only one thing – the 'present'. But what is the 'present'?

31. When we are pronouncing this word, the letters of this word which have been pronounced become past and the unpronounced letters still lie in the future. This means that only that sound which is being pronounced now is 'present'.

32. But of course the process of pronouncing this sound possesses a certain length. Consequently, a certain part of this process is 'present', just as the other parts are either past or future. But the same thing too may be said of this part of the process which had seemed to us to be 'the present'.

33. Reflecting in this manner, we see that there is no 'present'.

34. The present is only the 'impediment' in the transition from past to future and past and future appear to us as the *this* and *that* of the existence of time.

35. Thus: the present is the 'impediment' in the existence of time and, as we said earlier, space serves as the impediment in the existence of time.

36. By this means: the 'present' of time is space.

37. There is no space in the past and the future, it being contained entirely in the 'present'. And the present is space.

38. And since there is no present, neither is there any space.

39. We have explained the existence of time but space, of its own accord, does not yet exist.

40. In order to explain the existence of space, we must take that incidence when time performs as the impediment of space.

41. Experiencing the impediment of time, space splits into parts, generating the trinity of existence.

42. Broken down, existing space consists of three elements: *there*, *here* and *there*.

43. In the transition from one *there* to the other *there*, it is necessary to overcome the impediment *here*, because if it were not for the impediment *here*, then the one *there* and the other *there* would be unitary.

44. *Here* is the 'impediment' of existing space. And, as we said above, the impediment of existing space is time.

45. Therefore: the *here* of space is time.

46. The *here* of space and the 'present' of time are the points of intersection between time and space.

47. Examining space and time as basic elements in the existence of the universe, we would say: the universe expresses space, time and something else which is neither time nor space.

48. That 'something' which is neither time nor space is the 'impediment', which generates the existence of the universe.

49. This 'something' expresses the impediment between time and space.

50. Therefore this 'something' lies at the point of intersection of time and space.

51. Consequently this 'something' is to be found in time at the point of the 'present' and in space at the point of the 'here'.

52. This 'something' which is to be found at the point of intersection of space and time generates a certain 'impediment', separating the 'here' from the 'present'.

53. This 'something', generating the impediment and separating the 'here' from the 'present', creates a certain existence which we call matter or energy. (Henceforth we shall provisionally call this simply *matter*.)

54. Thus: the existence of the universe, as organized by space, time and their impediment, is expressed as *matter*.

55. Matter testifies to us of time.

56. Matter testifies to us of space.

57. By this means: the three basic elements of the existence of the universe are perceived by us as time, space and matter.

58. Time, space and matter, intersecting one with another at definite points and being basic elements in the existence of the universe, generate a certain node.

59. We shall call this node – the Node of the Universe.

60. When I say of myself: 'I am', I am placing myself within the Node of the Universe.

From 'A Tract More or Less According to a Synopsis of Emerson'

On an Approach to Immortality

It is peculiar to each person to strive for enjoyment, which is always either sexual satisfaction, or satiation, or acquisition.

But only that which lies not on the path to enjoyment leads towards immortality. All systems leading to immortality in the end come down to a single rule: *continually do that which you don't feel like doing*, because every person feels like either eating, or satisfying their sexual feelings, or acquiring something, or all of these more or less at a stroke. It is interesting that immortality is always connected with death and is treated by various religious systems as eternal enjoyment, or as eternal torment, or as an eternal absence of enjoyment and torment.

(1939)

LETTERS

Letter to the Lipavskys

28 June 1932. Tsarskoye Selo

Dear Tamara Aleksandrova and Leonid Savel'evich,
Thank you for your wonderful letter. I have re-read it many
times and learned it off by heart. I can be awakened in the
night and I will immediately and word-perfectly begin: 'Hello
there, Daniil Ivanovich, we are completely lost without you.
Lyonya has bought himself some new . . .' and so on, and so
on.

I have read this letter to all my acquaintances in Tsarskoye
Selo. Everyone likes it very much. Yesterday my friend Bal'nis
came to see me. He wanted to stay the night. I read him your
letter six times. He smiled very broadly, so it was evident that
he liked the letter, but he didn't have time to express a
detailed opinion, for he left without staying for the night.
Today I went round to his place myself and read the letter
through to him once more, so as to enable him to refresh his
memory. Then I asked Bal'nis for his opinion. But he broke a
leg off one of his chairs and with the aid of this leg he chased
me out on to the street and furthermore said that if I turn up
once more with this drivel he will tie my hands up and stuff
my mouth with muck from the rubbish pit. These were, of

course, on his part rather rude and po-faced remarks. I, of course, went away and took the view that he quite possibly had a bad cold and that he was not himself. From Bal'nis I went off to Yekaterinskiy Park and had a go on the rowing boats. On the whole lake, apart from me, there were two or three other boats. And, by the way, there was a very beautiful girl in one of the boats. And she was completely on her own. I turned my boat (incidentally, you have to row carefully when you're turning a boat, because the oars are liable to jump out of the rowlocks) and rowed after the beauty. I felt as though I resembled a Norwegian and I must have cut a fresh and healthy figure in my grey jacket and my fluttering tie and, as they say, had quite a whiff of the sea about me. But near the Orlov Column some hooligans were swimming and, as I rowed past, one of them just happened to have to swim right across my path. Then another of them shouted: – Wait a minute, while this blind and sweaty specimen goes past! – and pointed at me with his foot. This was very disagreeable because the beauty heard every word. And since she was rowing in front of me and in a rowing boat, as everyone knows, you sit with the back of your head towards your direction of movement, the beauty could not only hear, but she could see the hooligan pointing at me with his foot. I tried to make out that all this had nothing to do with me and started to look to the side with a smile on my face. But there wasn't a single other boat around. And at this point the hooligan shouted again: – Now what do you think you're looking at? We're talking to you, aren't we? Hey, you, the sucker in the cap!

I set about rowing with might and main, but the oars kept jumping out of the rowlocks and the boat only moved slowly. Finally, after an enormous effort, I caught up with the beauty and we got acquainted. She was called Yekaterina Pavlovna.

We took back her boat and Yekaterina Pavlovna moved over to mine. She turned out to be a very witty conversationalist. I had decided to dazzle my friends with wit, and so I got out your letter and made a start on reading it: 'Hello, there, Daniil Ivanovich, we are completely lost without you. Lyonya has bought himself some new ...' and so on. Yekaterina Pavlovna suggested that, if we pulled in to the bank, then I might see something. And I did, I saw Yekaterina Pavlovna making off, and out of the bushes there crept a filthy urchin, saying: – Mister, gie us a ride in yer boat.

This evening the letter came to grief. It happened like this: I was standing on the balcony, reading your letter and eating semolina. At that moment Auntie called me into the living room to help her wind the clock. I covered the semolina with the letter and went into the room. When I came back the letter had absorbed all the semolina into itself and I ate it.

The weather in Tsarskoye Selo is well set: variable cloud, south-west wind, possible rain.

This morning an organ-grinder came into our garden and played a trashy waltz, filched a hammock and ran away.

I read a very interesting book about how one young man fell in love with a certain young person, and this young person loved another young man, and this young man loved another young person and this young person loved another young man yet again, who loved not her but another young person.

And suddenly this young person stumbles down a trap-door and fractures her spine. But when she has completely recovered from that, she suddenly catches her death of cold and dies. Then the young man who loves her does himself in with a revolver shot. Then the young person who loves this young man throws herself under a train. Then the young man who loves this young person climbs up a tram pylon from grief and touches the live wire, dying from an electric shock. Then the young person who loves this young man stuffs herself with ground glass and dies from perforation of the intestines. Then the young man who loves this young person runs away to America and takes to the drink to such a degree that he sells his last suit and, for the lack of a suit, he is obliged to lie in hospital, where he suffers from bedsores, and from these bedsores he dies.

In a few days I shall be in town. I definitely want to see you. Give my best wishes to Valentina Yefimovna and Yakob Semyonovich.

Daniil Kharms

A Letter

Dear Nikandr Andreyevich,
I have received your letter and straight away I realized that it was from you. At first I thought that it might not be from you, but as soon as I unsealed it I immediately realized it was from you, though I had been on the point of thinking that it was not from you. I am glad that you, long ago now, got married, because when a person gets married to the one he wanted to marry, then this means he has got what he wanted. I am very glad you got married, because when a person marries the one he wanted to marry, that means he has got what he wanted. Yesterday I received your letter and immediately thought that this letter was from you, but then I thought that it

seemed not to be from you, but unsealed it and I see: it really is from you. You did exactly the right thing, writing to me. First you didn't write, and then you suddenly wrote, although before that, before that period when you didn't write, you also used to write. Immediately as I received your letter, I straight away decided that it was from you and, then, I was very glad that you had already got married. For, if a person should feel like getting married, then he really has to get married, come what may. Therefore I am very glad that you finally got married to the very one you wanted to marry. And you did exactly the right thing, writing to me. I was greatly cheered up on seeing your letter and I even immediately thought it was from you. It's true, while I was unsealing it, the thought did flash across my mind that it was not from you, but then, all the same, I decided it was from you. Thank you for writing. I am grateful to you for this and very glad for you. Perhaps you can't guess why I am so glad for you, but I will tell you at once that I am glad for you because you got married, and to the very one you wanted to marry. And, you know, it is very good to marry the very one you want to marry, because then you have got the very thing you wanted. It's for that very reason that I am so glad for you. But also I am glad because you wrote me a letter. I had even from some distance decided that the letter was from you, but as I took it in my hands I then thought: but what if it's not from you? But then I start to think: no, of course it's from you. I unseal the letter myself and at the same time I think: from you or not from you? From you or not from you? Well, as I unsealed it, then I could see: it's from you. I was greatly cheered and decided to write you a letter as well. There's a lot which has to be said, but literally there's no time. I have written what I had time to write in this letter and the rest I shall write another time, as now there really isn't time at all. It's a good thing, at least, that you wrote me a letter. Now I know that you got married a long time ago. I, from your previous letters too, knew that you had got married and now I see again: it's absolutely true, you have got married. And I'm very glad that you got married and wrote me a letter. I straight away, as soon as I saw your letter, decided that you had got married again. Well, I think it's a good thing that you have again got married and written me a letter about it. Now write to me and tell me who your new wife is and how it all came about. Say hello from me to your new wife.

Daniil Kharms
(1933)

Letter to K.V. Pugachova:
an Extract

I don't know the right word to express that strength in you which so delights me. I usually call it *purity*. I have been thinking about how beautiful everything is at first! How beautiful primary reality is! The sun and the grass are beautiful, grass and stone, and water, a bird, a beetle, a fly, and a human being (a kitten and a key, a comb). But if I were blind and deaf, had lost all my faculties, how could I know all this beauty? Everything gone and nothing for me at all. But I suddenly acquire touch and immediately almost the whole world appears again. I invent hearing and the world improves significantly. I invent all the other faculties and the world gets even bigger and better. The world starts to exist as soon as I let it in to me. Never mind its state of disorder, at least it exists! However, I started to bring some order into the world. And that's when Art appeared. Only at this point did I grasp the true difference between the sun and a comb but, at the same time, I realized that they are one and the same.

Now my concern is to create the correct order. I am carried away by this and only think of this. I speak about it, try to narrate it, describe it, sketch it, dance it, construct it. I am the creator of a world and this is the most important thing in me. How can I not think constantly about it! In everything I do, I invest the consciousness of being creator of a world. And I am not making simply some boot, but, first and foremost, I am creating something new. It doesn't bother me that the boot should turn out to be comfortable, durable and elegant. It's more important that it should contain that same order pertaining in the world as a whole, so that world order should not be the poorer, should not be soiled by contact with skin and nails, so that, notwithstanding the form of the boot, it should preserve its own form, should remain the same as it was, should remain *pure*.

It is that same purity which permeates all the arts. When I am writing poetry, the most important thing seems to me not the idea, not the content, and not the form, and not the misty conception of 'quality', but something even more misty and incomprehensible to the rationalistic mind, but comprehensible to me and, I hope, to you (. . .) – it is *the purity of order*.

This purity is one and the same – in the sun, in the grass, in a human being and in poetry. True art is on a par with primary reality; it creates a world and constitutes the world's primary reflection. It is indisputably real.

But, my God, what trivialities make up true art! *The Divine Comedy* is a great piece of work, but [Pushkin's] lines 'Through the agitated mists the moon makes its way' are no less great. For in both there is the same purity and consequently an identical proximity to reality, that is to independent existence. That means it is not simply words and thoughts printed on paper, but a piece of work which is just as real as the cut-glass bubble for the ink standing in front of me on the table. These verses seem to have become a piece of work which could be taken off the paper and hurled at the window, and the window would smash. That's what words can do!

But, on the other hand, how helpless and pitiful these same words can be! I never read the newspapers. They are a fictitious world, not the created one. Just pitiful, down-at-heel typographical print on rotten prickly paper.

Does a person need anything, apart from life and art? I don't think so: nothing else is needed, as everything genuine is to be found in them.

I think that purity can be in everything, even in the way a person eats soup.

(1933)

Letter to his Sister: Ye. I. Yuvachova

28 February, 1936

Dear Liza,
I convey my best wishes to Kirill on his birthday and similarly congratulate his parents on successfully fulfilling the plan

prescribed for them by nature for the raising up to the age of two years of human offspring, unable to walk, but therefore gradually beginning to destroy everything around and finally, in attaining this junior pre-school age, belabouring across the head with a voltmeter stolen from his father's writing table his loving mother, who has failed to evade the highly skilfully delivered assaults of her not as yet fully mature child, who is planning already in his immature skull, having done away with his parents, to direct all his most penetrating attentions towards his venerable grandfather and by the same means demonstrate a mental development allotted beyond his years, in honour of which, on the 28th of February, will gather a couple of admirers of this indeed outstanding phenomenon, among whose number, to my great chagrin, I shall not be able to be, finding myself at the time in question under a certain pressure, being enraptured on the shores of the Gulf of Finland by an ability, innate since childhood, of grabbing a steel pen and, having dipped it in an ink-well, in short sharp phrases expressing my profound and at times even in a certain way highly elevated thoughts.

Daniil Kharms

Letter to Aleksandr Vvedensky

Dear Aleksandr Ivanovich,
I have heard that you are saving money and have already saved thirty-five thousand. What for? Why save money? Why

not share what you have with those who do not even have a totally spare pair of trousers? I mean, what is money? I have studied this question. I possess photographs of the banknotes in widest circulation: to the value of a rouble, three, four and even five roubles. I have heard of banknotes of an intrinsic worth of up to 30 roubles at a time! But, as for saving them: what for? Well, I am not a collector. I have always despised collectors who amass stamps, feathers, buttons, onions and so on. They are stupid, dull superstitious people. I know for example that what are called 'numismatists' – that's those who accumulate coins – have the superstitious habit of putting them, have you ever thought where? Not on the table, not in a box, but ... on their books! What do you think of that? Whereas money can be picked up, taken to a shop and exchanged, well ... let's say for soup (that's a kind of food), or for grey-mullet sauce (that's also a kind of foodstuff).

No, Aleksandr Ivanovich, you are almost as couth a person as I, yet you save money and don't change it into a range of other things. Forgive me, dear Aleksandr Ivanovich, but that is not terribly clever! You've simply gone a little stupid living out there in the provinces. There must be no one to talk to, even. I'm sending you my picture so that you will be able at least to see before you a clever, cultivated, intellectual, first-rate face.

Your friend Daniil Kharms
(Late 1930s)

Autobiographical Writings

[How I Was Born]

Now I will describe how I was born, how I grew up and how the first signs of genius were discovered in me. I was born twice. This is how it happened.

My Dad got married to my Mum in 1902, but my parents brought me into the world only at the end of 1905, because Dad was adamant that his child should be born at New Year. Dad calculated that conception had to take place on the first of April and only on that day did he get round my Mum with the proposition of conceiving a child.

My Dad got round my Mum on the first of April 1903. Mum had long been awaiting this moment and was terribly thrilled. But Dad, as it seems, was in a very playful mood and could not restrain himself, saying to Mum: 'April Fool!'.

Mum was absolutely furious and didn't allow Dad anywhere near her that day. There was nothing for it but to wait until the following year.

On the first of April 1904, Dad again started getting round Mum with the same proposition. But Mum, remembering what had happened the year before, said that she had no further desire to be left in that stupid position and again would not allow Dad near her. It didn't matter how much Dad created, it got him nowhere.

And only a year later did my Dad manage to have his way with my Mum and beget me.

And so my conception took place on the first of April 1905.

However, all Dad's calculations broke down because I turned out to be premature and was born four months before my time.

Dad created such a fuss that the midwife who had delivered me lost her head and started to shove me back in, from where I had only just emerged.

An acquaintance of ours who was in attendance, a student from the military medical academy, declared that shoving me back in would not work. However, the student's words notwithstanding, they still shoved me and shoved me back, for all they were worth.

At this point a fearful commotion broke out.

The progenetrix yells: – Give me my baby!

And the response comes: – Your baby – they tell her – is inside you.

– What! – yells the progenetrix. – How can my baby be inside me when I have just given birth to him!

– But – they say to the progenetrix – mightn't you be mistaken?

– What! – yells the progenetrix – mistaken? How can I be mistaken! I saw the baby myself, he was lying here on a sheet only just now!

– That is true – they tell the progenetrix – but perhaps he's crawled off somewhere. – In a word, they themselves don't know what to tell the progenetrix.

And the progenetrix is still making a noise and demanding her baby.

There was nothing for it, but to call an experienced doctor. The experienced doctor examined the progenetrix and threw up his hands; however, he thought it all out and gave the progenetrix a good dose of English salts, and by this means I saw the light of day for the second time.

At this juncture, Dad again started creating a fuss, saying that, surely, this couldn't be called a birth, that this, surely, couldn't yet be called a human being, but rather a semi-foetus, and that it ought to either be shoved back again or put into a incubator.

And so they put me into an incubator.

(1935)

The Incubating Period

I sat in the incubator for four months. I remember only that the incubator was made of glass, was transparent and had a thermometer. I sat inside the incubator on cotton wool. I don't remember anything else about it.

After four months they took me out of the incubator. They did this, as it happens, on the first of January 1906.

By this means, I was to all intents and purposes born for a third time.

But it was the first of January that was counted as my birthday.

(1935)

Note
Daniil Kharms was in fact born on 17 December (Old Style) / 30 December (New Style), 1905.

Memoirs

[I Decided to Mess Up the Party . . .]

1.

Once I arrived at Gosizdat [publishing house] and met in Gosizdat Yevgeniy L'vovich Shvarts who, as always, was badly dressed but with pretentions to something.

Catching sight of me, Shvarts began to crack jokes but also, as always, unsuccessfully.

I cracked jokes significantly more successfully and soon, with regard to intellectual relations, put Shvarts squarely on his back.

Everyone around envied my wit, but they could do nothing about it as they literally killed themselves laughing. In particular Nina Vladimirovna Gernet and David Yefimych Rakhmilovich, who called himself Eugene because of the sound of it, used to kill themselves laughing.

Seeing that his jokes didn't work with me, Shvarts started to change his tone and in the end, cursing me up and down, declared that everyone in Tiflis knows Zabolotsky and hardly anyone knows me.

At this point I lost my temper and said that I was more historically important than Shvarts and Zabolotsky, that I shall leave a radiant mark upon history and that they will quickly be forgotten.

Having got the feel of my magnitude and my major world significance, Shvarts gradually began to palpitate and invited me round for dinner.

2.

I decided to mess up the party, and that's what I'm going to do.

I'll start with Valentina Yefimovna. This inhospitable personage invites us round and instead of a meal she puts on the table some awful sour stuff. I enjoy eating and I know what's what when it comes to food. You can't fool me with sour muck! I even go into restaurants on occasions and see what sort of food they have there. And I cannot stand it when this particularity of my character is not recognized.

Now I'll move on to Leonid Savel'evich Lipavsky. He didn't shrink from telling me to my face that every month he composes ten thoughts.

In the first place, he's lying. He doesn't have ten ideas, it's less.

And secondly, I think up more. I haven't counted up how many I think up in a month, but it must be more than he does ...

And I, for example, don't throw it in everyone's face that I, so to speak, possess a colossal mind. I have quite sufficient evidence to consider myself a great man. Yes and, by the way, I do consider myself such.

Therefore it is insulting and painful for me to find myself among people who are inferior to me in terms of mind, insight and talent, and not to feel that I am accorded the respect that is fully my due.

Why, oh why am I better than everyone else?

3.

Now I have understood everything: Leonid Savel'evich is a German. He even has German habits. Look at the way he eats. Well, he's pure German and that's all there is to it. Even by his legs you can tell that he's a German.

Without boasting at all, I am able to say that I am very observant and witty.

So, for example, if you take Leonid Savel'evich, Yuriy Berzin and Vol'f Erlikh and line them all up together on the pavement, then you could well call them: major, minor and minimus.

In my view that's witty, because it's moderately funny.

And all the same, Leonid Savel'evich is a German! I really must tell him this when I see him.

I don't consider myself an especially intelligent person, but all the same I have to say that I'm more intelligent than the rest. Perhaps there's someone more intelligent than me on Mars, but I don't know about on Earth.

For instance, they say that Oleinikov is very intelligent. And in my view he is intelligent, but not very. He discovered, for example, that if you write a '6' and turn it upside down, then you get a '9'. And in my view that's just stupid.

Leonid Savel'evich is absolutely right when he says that someone's mind is their worth. And if there is no mind, that means there is no worth.

Yakov Semyonovich argues with Leonid Savel'evich and says that someone's mind is their weakness. And in my view that's already a paradox. Why ever should the mind be a weakness? Not at all. Rather, it's a stronghold. I think so, anyway.

We often get together at Leonid Savel'evich's and talk about this. If an argument breaks out, then I always turn out the winner of the argument. I don't know why myself.

Everyone regards me with a certain astonishment, for some reason. Whatever I do, everyone finds it astonishing.

I don't even make any effort. Everything seems to work out of its own accord.

Zabolotsky said some time that I was born to govern the

spheres. He must have been joking. No such idea has ever entered my head.

In the Writers' Union I am considered an angel, for some reason.

Listen, my friends! In fact you shouldn't bend the knee before me like that. I am just the same as all of you, only better.

4.

I have heard the phrase: 'Seize the moment!'.

It's easily said, but hard to do. In my view, it's a meaningless expression. And really, you can't call for the impossible.

I say this with complete certainty, because I have tested everything on myself. I have grabbed at the moment but not managed to seize it and have merely broken my watch. Now I know that it's impossible.

It's also impossible to 'seize the epoch', because it's the same as the moment, only a bit more so.

It's another matter if you say: 'document what is happening at this moment' ... That is quite another matter.

So, for example: one, two, three! Nothing happened! And so I have documented a moment in which nothing happened.

I told Zabolotsky about this. He was very taken by this and sat the whole day counting: one, two, three! I made notes that nothing had happened.

Shvarts caught Zabolotsky at this activity. And Shvarts also took an interest in this original means of documenting what was happening in our epoch, since an epoch is formed out of moments.

But I beg to draw your attention to the fact that once again I was the prime mover of this method. Me again! Me everywhere! It's simply astonishing!

What comes with difficulty to others comes easily to me!

I can even fly. But I'm not going to tell you about that because, come what may, nobody will believe it.

5.

Whenever two people are playing chess, it always seems to me that one is fooling the other. Especially if they are playing for money.

In general, I find any kind of playing for money disgusting. I forbid gambling in my presence.

And as for card players, I would have them executed. That would be the best method of getting to grips with games of chance.

Instead of playing card games, it would be better if people would get together and read each other a bit of ethics.

Though ethics is rather boring. Womanizing is more fun.

Women have always interested me. Women's legs have always excited me, especially above the knee.

Many people consider women to be depraved creatures. But not me! On the contrary, I even consider them to be somehow quite pleasant.

A plumpish young woman! What's depraved about her? She's not depraved at all!

Children are another matter. They are usually said to be innocent. And I consider that they might well be innocent, but anyway they are highly loathsome, especially when they are dancing. I always make an exit from anywhere where there are children.

Leonid Savel'evich also doesn't like children. And it was me who inspired him with such ideas.

Generally speaking, everything that Leonid Savel'evich says has already been said at some time by me.

And that doesn't only go for Leonid Savel'evich.

Everyone is only too pleased to pick up even scraps of my

ideas. I even find this funny.

For example, Oleinikov ran up to me yesterday, saying that he had got into a complete muddle over questions of existence. I gave him some sort of advice and discharged him. He went off delighted with me and in his very best mood.

People see me as a means of support, they repeat my words, they are astonished by my actions, but they don't pay me money.

Foolish people! Bring me a bit more money and you will see how pleased that will make me.

6.
Now I'll say a few words about Aleksandr Ivanovich [Vvedensky].

He's a wind-bag and a card player. But what I value him for is his obedience to me.

By day and by night he dances attendance on me, just waiting for a hint from me of some command. I have only to proffer such a hint and Aleksandr Ivanovich flies like the wind to carry out my wish.

For this I bought him some shoes and said: – There you are, wear them! And so he wears them.

Whenever Aleksandr Ivanovich arrives at Gosizdat, they all laugh and say to each other that Aleksandr Ivanovich has come for his money.

Konstantin Ignat'evich Drovatsky hides under the table. I say this in an allegorical sense.

More than anything, Aleksandr Ivanovich loves macaroni. He always eats it with ground rusks and he gobbles up almost a whole kilo, and perhaps even much more.

Having eaten his macaroni, Aleksandr Ivanovich says he feels sick and lies down on the divan. Sometimes the macaroni comes back up.

Aleksandr Ivanovich doesn't eat meat and he doesn't like women. Although sometimes he likes them. Apparently, even very often.

But the women whom Aleksandr Ivanovich likes, to my taste, are all ugly, and therefore we shall consider that they are not even women at all.

If I say a thing, that means it's correct.

I don't advise anyone to argue with me, as they will just be made a fool of, because I get the last word with everyone.

And it's no use you bandying words with me. That's already been tried. I've seen them all off! Never mind that I don't look as though I can talk, but when I get going, there's no stopping me.

Once I got going at the Lipavskys and that was that! I talked them all to death!

Then I went off to the Zabolotskys and talked everyone's head off there. Then I went to the Shvartses and talked everyone's head off there. Then I arrived home and talked half the night away again there!

(1930s)

EROTICA

[I Love Sensual Women]

I love sensual women and not passionate ones. A passionate woman closes her eyes, moans and shouts and the enjoyment of a passionate woman is blind. A passionate woman writhes about, grabs you with her hands without looking where, clasps you, kisses you, even bites you and hurries to reach her climax as soon as she can. She has no time to display her sexual organs, no time to examine, touch with the hand and kiss your sexual organs, she is in such a hurry to slake her passion. Having slaked her passion, the passionate woman will fall asleep. The sexual organs of a passionate woman are dry. A passionate woman is always in some way or another mannish.

The sensual woman is always feminine.

Her contours are rounded and abundant.

The sensual woman rarely reaches a blind passion. She savours sexual enjoyment. The sensual woman is always a woman and even in an unaroused state her sexual organs are moist. She has to wear a bandage on her sexual organs, so as not to soak them with moisture.

When she takes the bandage off in the evening, the bandage is so wet that it can be squeezed out.

Thanks to such an abundance of juices, the sexual organs

of a sensual woman give off a slight, pleasant smell which increases strongly when the sensual woman is aroused. Then the juice from her sexual organs is secreted in a syrupy stream.

A sensual woman likes you to examine her sexual organs.

(early 1930s)

Foma Bobrov and his Spouse

A Comedy in Three Parts

GRANNY BOBROV (*Playing patience*) Now that's the card. Oh, it's all coming out topsy-turvy! A king. And where am I supposed to put that? Just when you want one, there's never a five around. Oh, I could do with a five! Now it'll be the five. Oh, sod it, another king!

She flings the cards on to the table with such force that a porcelain vase falls off the table and smashes.

GRANNY Oh! Oh! My Gawd! These bloody cards! (*She crawls under the table and picks up the pieces*). This'll never glue back together again. And it was a good vase, too. You can't get them like that any more. This bit's right over there! (*Stretches for the piece.* BOBROV *enters the room*).

BOBROV Granny! Is that you clambering about

217

	under the table?
GRANNY	Yes, okay, okay. What do you want?
BOBROV	I just came to ask you: you wouldn't happen to have a chest of tea?
GRANNY	Come on then, give me a hand up from under the table.
BOBROV	What have you done, dropped something? Oh, you've broken the vase!
GRANNY	(*Mimicking him*) You've broken the vase! (BOBROV *helps* GRANNY *up. But as soon as he lets go of her,* GRANNY *sits back down on the floor*).
BOBROV	Oh, you're down again!
GRANNY	Down, so now what?
BOBROV	Let me help you up (*Pulls* GRANNY *up*).
GRANNY	The cards were going badly. I tried this and that . . . But don't pull me by the arms, get hold of me under the armpits. All I got, you know, was king after king. I need a five and all the kings keep turning up.

BOBROV *lets go of* GRANNY *and* GRANNY *again sprawls on the floor.*

GRANNY	Akh!
BOBROV	Oh, Lord! You're down again.
GRANNY	What are you on about: down, down! What are you after, anyway?
BOBROV	I came to ask if you've a chest of tea.
GRANNY	I know that. You've already told me. I don't like listening to the same tale twenty times. The thing is: akh, I'm down again! and a chest of tea. Well, what are you looking at! Get me up, I'm telling you.
BOBROV	(*Pulling* GRANNY *up*) I'll just, excuse me, put

you in the armchair.

GRANNY   You'd do better to prattle on a bit less and pull me up in a proper fashion. I meant to tell you, and it almost slipped my mind: you know, that door in my bedroom isn't shutting properly again. No doubt you messed the whole thing up.

BOBROV   No, I put a staple on with fillister-head screws.

GRANNY   Do you think I know anything about staples and fillister heads? I don't care about all that. I just want the door to shut.

BOBROV   It doesn't shut properly because the fillister heads won't stay in the woodwork.

GRANNY   That'll do, that'll do. That's your business. I just need to ... Akh (*She again sprawls on the floor*).

BOBROV   Oh, Lord!

GRANNY   Have you decided to fling me to the floor deliberately? Decided to have a bit of fun? Oh you useless devil! You're just a useless devil and you might as well clear off!

BOBROV   No, Granny, 'onest injun, I just meant to put you in the armchair.

GRANNY   Did you hear what I said? I told you to clear out! So why aren't you going? Well, why aren't you going? Do you hear? Clear off out of it! Well? Bugger off! (*Exit* BOBROV).

GRANNY   Off! Go on! Away! Bugger off! Talk about a reprobate! (*Gets up from the floor and sits in the armchair*). And his wife is simply an indecent madam. The madam walks about absolutely starkers and doesn't bat an eyelid, even in front of me, an old woman. She covers her indecent patch with the palm of her hand, and that's the way she walks around. And then she touches the bread with that hand at lunchtime. It's simply revolting to watch. She thinks that if she's young and pretty, then she can do anything she likes. And as for herself, the trollop, she never washes herself properly just where she should do. I, she says, like a whiff of woman to come from a woman! And as for me, as soon as I see her coming, I'm straight into the bathroom with the eau de Cologne to my nose. Perhaps it may be nice for men, but as for me, you can spare me that. The shameless hussy! She goes around naked without the slightest embarrassment. And when she sits down she doesn't even keep her legs together properly, so that everything's on show. And – there, she's well just always wet. She's secreting like that all the time. If you tell her she should go and wash herself, she will say you shouldn't wash there too often and she'll take a handkerchief and just wipe herself. And you're lucky if it's a handkerchief, because just with her hand she smears it all over the place. I never give her my hand, as there's perpetually an indecent smell from her hands. And her breasts are indecent. It's true, they are very fine and bouncy, but they are so big that, in my opinion, they're simply indecent. That's

the wife that Foma found for himself! How
she ever got round him is beyond me.

(1933)

Disarmed, or Unfortunate in Love

A Tragic Vaudeville in One Act

LEV MARKOVICH   (*Bounding up to the* LADY) Let me!
LADY   (*Keeping him at arms length*) Leave me!
LEV MARKOVICH   (*Bumping into her*) Let me!
LADY   (*Shoving him with her knees*) Go away!
LEV MARKOVICH   (*Gripping her with his hands*) Let's, just once!
LADY   (*Shoving him with her knees*) Away! Away!
LEV MARKOVICH   Just one thrust!
LADY   (*Bellowing*) No-o.
LEV MARKOVICH   A thrust! One thrust!
LADY   (*Shows the whites of her eyes*).

LEV MARKOVICH *fumbles around, reaches with his hand for his tool
and suddenly, as it turns out, he can't find it.*

LEV MARKOVICH   Wait a minute! (*Feels himself up and down with
his hands*). What the h-hell!

LADY *looks at* LEV MARKOVICH *with astonishment.*

LEV MARKOVICH   Well, that's a damn funny thing!

LADY   What's happened?

LEV MARKOVICH   Hum ... hmm ... (*Looks around, completely flummoxed*).

(*Curtain*)

(*1934*)

[But the Artist]

But the artist sat the nude model on the table and moved her legs apart. The girl hardly resisted and merely covered her face with her hands.

Amonova and Strakhova said that first the girl should have been taken off to the bathroom and washed between her legs, as any whiff of such an aroma was simply repulsive. The girl wanted to jump up but the artist held her back and asked her to take no notice and sit there, just as he had placed her. The girl, not knowing what she was supposed to do, sat back down again. The artist and his female colleagues took their respective seats and began sketching the nude model. Petrova said that the nude model was a very seductive woman, but Strakhova and Amonova said that she was rather plump and indecent. Zolotogromov said that this was what made her seductive, but Strakhova said that this was simply repulsive, and not at all seductive.

– Look, – Strakhova, – ugh! It's pouring out of her on to the table cloth. What is there seductive about that, when I can sniff the smell off her from here.

Petrova said that this only showed her feminine strength. Abel'far blushed and agreed. Amonova said she had seen nothing like it, that you get to the highest point of arousal and it still wouldn't secrete like this girl did. Petrova said that, faced with that, one could get aroused oneself and that Zolotogromov must already be aroused.

Zolotogromov agreed that the girl was having quite an effect on him. Abel'far sat there red in the face and she was breathing heavily.

– However, the air in this room is becoming unbearable! – said Strakhova. Abel'far fidgeted on her chair and then leapt up and went out of the room.

– There – said Petrova – you see the result of female seductiveness. It even acts on the ladies. Abel'far has gone off to put herself to rights. I can feel that I will soon have to do the same thing.

– That – said Amonova – only shows the advantage we thin women possess. Everything with us is always as it should be. But both you and Abel'far are splendiferous ladies and you have to keep yourselves very much in check.

– Yet – said Zolotogromov – splendiferousness and a certain lack of bodily hygiene are what is to be particularly valued in a woman.

(1934–1937)

How a Man Crumbled

– They say all the best tarts are fat-arsed. Ee-ee, I really like busty tarts, I love the way they smell.

Having said this, he started to increase in height and, upon reaching the ceiling, he crumbled into a thousand little pellets. The yard-keeper Panteley came, swept all these pellets up into his scoop, in which he normally picked up the horse muck, and he carried these pellets away somewhere to the back yard.

And the sun continued to shine as ever and splendiferous ladies continued to smell just as ravishingly as ever.

(1936)

[I didn't go in for . . .]

I didn't go in for blocking up my ears. Everyone blocked theirs up and I alone didn't block mine and therefore I alone heard everything. Similarly, I didn't blindfold myself with a rag, as everyone else did, and therefore I saw everything. Yes, I alone saw and heard everything. But unfortunately I didn't understand anything and, therefore, what was the value of me alone seeing and hearing everything? I couldn't even remember what I had seen and heard. Just a few fragmentary recollections, flourishes and nonsensical sounds. There was a tram conductor who came running through, followed by an elderly lady with a spade between her lips. Someone said: 'it's probably from under her chair'. A naked Jewish girl spreads her legs and empties a cup of milk over her sexual organs, the milk trickles down into a deep dinner plate. From the plate, the milk is poured back into the cup and offered to me to drink. I take a drink: there is a cheesy smell from the milk . . .

The naked Jewish girl is sitting there before me with her legs apart, her sexual organs stained with milk. She leans forward and looks at her sexual organs. From her sexual organs there starts to flow a transparent and syrupy liquid ... I am going through a big and rather dark yard. In the yard there lie high, heaped up piles of firewood. From behind the wood someone's face is looking out. I know: it's Limonin following me. He's on the watch: to see whether I'm going to visit his wife. I turn to the right and go through the outside door on to the street. From the gateway the joyful face of Limonin is looking out ... And now Limonin's wife is offering me vodka. I down four glasses with a few sardines and start thinking about the naked Jewish girl. Limonin's wife puts her head on my knees. I knock back one more glass and light up my pipe.

– You are so sad today. – Limonin's wife says to me. I tell her some nonsense or other and go off to the Jewish girl.

(1940)

Postscript
by Neil Cornwell

Daniil Kharms
(1905-1942)

Russian literature seems always able to bring forth new, interesting writers who are experimenting somewhere at the frontiers of literary style, language or story. Among our contemporaries (and near contemporaries), we may think of Andrey Siniavsky (alias 'Abram Tertz'), Vasiliy Aksyonov, Sasha Sokolov and Yevgeniy Popov, as well as the more recent Victor Pelevin and Valeriy Ronshin, along perhaps with the women writers who emerged under *glasnost'* during the last Soviet years: Lyudmilla Petrushevskaya, Tatyana Tolstaya and others. But alongside the new writers, we have long continued to re-discover the old. Mikhail Bulgakov and Andrey Platonov, unexpected jewels from the Stalinist period, only came to prominence decades after their own time. The most recent re-discovery is Sigizmund Krzhizhanovsky (1887-1950), whose collected *Seven Stories* has recently appeared in Joanne Turnbull's English translation (published by Glas, 2006). Discoveries from the 'Silver Age' period are still coming, or returning, to light. Neglected figures from even further back are still achieving or recovering a belated but deserved readership (Vladimir Odoevsky from the Romantic period; Vsevolod Garshin from later in the nineteenth century). Another fascinating figure, the contemporary of Bulgakov, Platonov and Krzhizhanovsky, and with an even greater resonance for the modern, or indeed the postmodern, world is Daniil Kharms.

'Daniil Kharms' was the main, and subsequently the sole, pen-name of Daniil Ivanovich Iuvachov. The son of a St Petersburg political, religious and literary figure, Daniil was to achieve limited local renown only – as a Leningrad avant-garde eccentric and a writer of children's stories in the 1920s and 30s. Among other pseudonyms, he had employed 'Daniil Dandan' and 'Kharms-Shardarm'. The predilection for 'Kharms' is thought to derive from appreciation of the tension between the English words 'charms' and 'harms' (plus the German *Charme*; indeed, there is an actual German surname 'Harms'), but may also owe something to a similarity in sound to Sherlock Holmes (pronounced 'Kholms' in Russian) – a figure of considerable fascination to Kharms.

From 1925 Kharms began to appear at poetry readings and other avant-garde activities, gained membership of the Leningrad section of the All-Russian Union of Poets (from 1926), one of the many predecessors to the eventual Union of Soviet Writers, and published two poems in anthologies in 1926 and 1927. Almost unbelievably now, these were the only 'adult' works Kharms was able to publish in his lifetime. In 1927 Kharms joined together with a number of like-minded experimental writers, including his talented friend and close associate Aleksandr Vvedensky (1904-1941) and the major poet Nikolay Zabolotsky (1903-1958), to form the literary and artistic grouping *OBERIU* (the near-acronym of the 'Association of Real Art').

Representing something of a union between Futurist aesthetics and Formalist approaches, the Oberiuty considered themselves a 'left flank' of the literary avant-garde. Their publicity antics, including roof-top appearances by Kharms, caused minor sensations and they succeeded in presenting a highly unconventional theatrical evening entitled 'Three Left Hours' in 1928, which included the performance of Kharms's Kafkaesque absurdist drama *Yelizaveta Bam*. Among the *OBERIU* catch-phrases were 'Art is a cupboard' (Kharms normally made his theatrical entrances inside or on a wardrobe) and 'Poems aren't pies, we aren't herring'. However, the time for propagating experimental modernist art, in the Stalinizing years of the late 1920s, had passed. The rising Soviet neo-bourgeoisie were not to be shocked: tolerance of any such frivolities was plummeting as fast as Kharms's old women, and hostile journalistic attention ensured the hurried disbandment of the *OBERIU* group, following a number of further appearances.

Kharms and Vvedensky evidently felt it wiser to allow themselves to be drawn into the realm of children's literature, writing for publications of the children's publishing house Detgiz, known fondly as the 'Marshak Academy', being run by the redoubtable children's writer (and bowdlerizer of Robbie Burns), Samuil Marshak, and involving too the playwright Yevgeniy Shvarts. By 1940 Kharms had published eleven children's books and contributed regularly to the magazines *The Hedgehog* and *The Siskin*. However, even in this field of literary activity, anything out of the ordinary was not safe. Kharms, in his playful approach to children's writing, utilised a number of *OBERIU*-type devices. The *OBERIU* approach had been denounced in a Leningrad paper in 1930 as 'reactionary sleight-of-hand' and, at the end of 1931 Kharms and Vvedensky were arrested, accused of 'deflecting the people from the building of socialism by means of trans-sense verses' and exiled to Kursk. However the exile was fairly brief, the times then being what Anna Akhmatova described as 'relatively vegetarian'. Nevertheless, little work was to be had thereafter; fluctuations in favour at Detgiz and periods of near-starvation followed. Kharms and Vvedensky (the latter had moved to the Ukraine in the mid-1930s) survived the main purges of the 1930s. However, the outbreak of war brought new dangers: Kharms was arrested in Leningrad in August 1941, while Vvedensky's arrest took place the following month in Kharkov.

Vvedensky died in December of that year and Kharms (it seems of starvation in prison hospital) in February 1942, Both were subsequently 'rehabilitated' during the Khrushchev 'Thaw', but most of their adult writings had to await the Gorbachev period for publication in Russia.

Both starvation and arrest were anticipated in a number of Kharms's writings. Hunger and poverty were constant companions; indeed, Kharms can lay claim to being the poet of hunger (not for nothing did he take strongly to Knut Hamsun's novel of that name), as the following translation of an unrhyming but rhythmic verse fragment shows:

> This is how hunger begins:
> The morning you wake, feeling lively,
> Then begins the weakness,
> Then begins the boredom;
> Then comes the loss
> Of the power of quick reason,
> Then comes the calmness
> And then begins the horror.

On his general situation in life, Kharms wrote the following quatrain in 1937:

> We've had it now in life's realm,
> Of all hope we are now bereft.
> Gone is happiness's dream,
> Destitution is all that's left.

The arrest of Kharms came, reportedly, when the caretaker of the block of flats in which he lived called him down, in his bedroom slippers, 'for a few minutes'. He was apparently charged with spreading defeatist propaganda: there is evidence that, even at the time, he managed to clear himself of this charge, possibly by feigning insanity.

Kharms had been a marked man since his first arrest in 1931 and he was probably lucky to escape disaster over the children's poem in 1937, about a man who went out to buy tobacco and disappeared – 'Out of a house walked a man', later adapted by Aleksandr Galich into a song about Kharms himself. In addition, his first wife, Ester Rusakova, was a member of a well-known old émigré revolutionary family, subsequently purged; it is intriguing to recall that Kharms was, for several years, Victor Serge's brother-in-law.

By the 1930s Kharms was concentrating more on prose. In addition to his only then publishable works, his children's stories and verse, he evolved, 'for his draw', his own idiosyncratic brands of short prose and dramatic fragment. Theoretical, philosophical and even mathematical pieces were also penned, as well as diaries and notebooks, together with a sizeable body of poetry. The boundaries between genres are fluid with Kharms, as are distinctions between fragment and whole, finished and unfinished states. Most of Kharms's manuscripts were preserved after his arrest by his friend, the philosopher Yakov Druskin, until they could be safely handed on to reliable scholars or deposited in libraries. It comes as no surprise to anyone with the least inkling of Soviet literary conditions in the 1930s that these writings were then totally unpublishable – and indeed that their author is unlikely to have even contemplated trying to publish them. What is much more surprising is that they were written at all.

From 1962 the children's works of Kharms began to be reprinted in the Soviet Union. Isolated first publications of a few of his short humorous pieces for adults followed slowly thereafter, as did mentions of Kharms in memoirs. Only when Gorbachev's policy of *glasnost'* took real effect though, from 1987, did the flood of publications begin, including a major book-length collection in 1988. Abroad, an awareness of Kharms and the Oberiuty began to surface in the late 1960s, both in Eastern Europe and in the West, where a first collection in Russian appeared in 1974. In 1978 an annotated, but somewhat discontinuous, collected works of Kharms began to appear, published in Bremen by the Verlag K-Presse (appropriately enough, the 'Kafka Press'), edited from Leningrad. Four volumes (the poetic opus) appeared. It is presumably safe to assume that virtually all of Kharms's surviving works are now known, given the publication of what is claimed to be a *Full Collected Works* (six volumes, St Petersburg, 1997-2002).

A relatively recent 'find' is a selection of rather mild erotica, largely clinically voyeuristic and olfactory in nature, which suitably counterpoints certain tendencies already noticeable in some of Kharms's more mainstream writing.

The English or American reader may have come across some of Kharms's work in the anthologies published from 1971 by George Gibian, but more recently (surprisingly enough) in *New American Writing* (Number 20, 2002), developed into a new anthology, *OBERIU: An Anthology of Russian Absurdism* (see 'Further Reading', following this Postscript) – which avoids duplicating the material included in either Gibian's volume or in the present collection. The present translator's earlier (and briefer) selection of Kharms, entitled *The Plummeting Old Women* (The Lilliput Press, Dublin, 1989), was incorporated into the first edition of the present volume (along with much additional material). In addition to translations (into English, German and Italian, at least), a surrealistic film by Slobodan Pe?i? entitled *Slu?aj Harms* (*The Kharms Case*) was the Yugolsav entry at the 1988 Cannes Film Festival. In Russia OBERIU evenings and Kharms shows and 'monospectaculars' have become commonplace; *Moscow News* (even back in 1988, in its Russian and English issues alike) was proclaiming Kharms 'an international figure'. In recent years Kharmsian ballets, operas (notably the 'music dramas' of Haflidi Hallgrimsson), theatricals and other forms of show, whether in Russia or here and there in the West (as evidenced by Simon McBurney's 'Introduction' to this new edition of the present volume), have become almost commonplace – at least within certain cult circles. The 'art-folk-punk' Dutch pop group De Kift have recently turned their attention to songs based on poems by Kharms. In the present age of postmodernist fragmentation, Kharms's time has surely come.

On the assumption that Kharms's published *oeuvre* should now be complete, overall assessments of his achievement are assuming greater validity. Definitive texts from archival sources, in quite a number of instances, have replaced dubious variants. We know the intended order and content of the 'Incidents' (*Sluchai*) cycle, which was presented as a complete entity for the first time in English in the first edition of this collection. Many of the later examples of Kharms's short prose, written around 1940, only found publication in relatively recent years, along with the notebooks and letters.

The prose miniature, indeed, has long been a genre rather more commonly found in Russian literature than elsewhere. Among the disparate examples that come to mind (many of them by authors very different from Kharms) we may mention, from the nineteenth century: the *feuilletons* of writers such as Dostoevsky, the prose poems of Turgenev and the shortest of the fictional works by Garshin and Chekhov; and, from the twentieth, short pieces by Zamyatin, Olesha and Zoshchenko and, more recently, the aphoristic writings of Abram Tertz and the prose poems of Solzhenitsyn. In spirit, Kharms clearly belongs to a tradition of double-edged humour, extending from the word-play and irrelevancy of Gogol and the jaundiced mentality of Dostoevsky's 'underground' anti-heroes to the intertextual parody of Tertz and the satirical absurd of Voinovich. As suggested, Kharms has clear affinities with certain of the experimental Soviet writings that sprang from a Futurist-Formalist base in the 1920s.

In a verse and prose sequence entitled 'The Sabre' (*Sablya* of 1929), Kharms singles out for special admiration Goethe, Blake, Lomonsov, Gogol, Kozma Prutkov and Khlebnikov. In a diary entry of 1937, he lists as his 'favourite writers': Gogol, Prutkov, Meyrink, Hamsun, Edward Lear and Lewis Carroll. Such listings are revealing in determining Kharms's pedigree. On a general European level, Kharms had obvious affinities with the various modernist, Dadaist, surrealist, absurdist and other avant-garde movements. Borges wrote brief masterpieces, but in a rather different vein. Arguably, Kafka and Beckett provide closer parallels, while both Hamsun and Meyrink furnished Kharms with certain motifs. Some of the postmodernist minimalist writings of more recent decades are probably closer than anything else.

The Old Woman' (*Starukha*, 1939), a story reaching almost epic proportions by Kharms's standards, has strong claims to be regarded as his masterpiece. A deceptively multilayered story, this work looks simultaneously back to the Petersburg tradition of Russian story-telling and forward to the metafictional devices of our post-war era. 'Incidents' signals a neo-romantic concern with the relationship between the fragment and the whole (observable too in the theoretical pieces) and, now in its 'complete' form, it attracts critical interpretation as an entity in itself. The 'assorted stories', arranged chronologically, indicate the development of Kharms's idiosyncratic preoccupations over the decade from the early 1930s. *Yelizaveta Bam* represents Kharms's contribution to the theatre of the absurd. The remaining non-fictional and assorted pieces give an idea of Kharms's excursions into other forms of writing. Not included as such in this collection are his poetry and his children's writing.

If Kharms still seems somehow different from all previous models or comparisons, or more startling, this is perhaps most readily explicable by his constant adoption, at various levels, of what might be termed a poetics of extremism. Take, for example, his brevity: not for nothing did he note in his diary: 'garrulity is the mother of mediocrity'. If certain stories included here (especially some from 'Incidents') seem micro-texts of concise inconsequentiality, there remain others which incommode the printer even less: consider, for instance, the following 'complete' story:

> An old man was scratching his head with both hands. In
> places where he couldn't reach with both hands, he
> scratched himself with one, but very, very, fast. And while
> he was doing it he blinked rapidly.

Another feature of Kharmsian extremism resides in his uncompromising quest for the means to undermine his own stories, or to facilitate their self-destruction; there are numerous examples of this in the texts collected here.

Kharms, then, turns his surgical glance on both the extraordinary world of Stalin's Russia and on representation, past and present, in story-telling and other artistic forms. He thus operates, typically, against a precise Leningrad background. He reflects aspects of Soviet life and its literary forms, passing sardonic and despairing comment on the period in which he lived. He also ventures, ludicrously, into historical areas, parodying the ways in which respected worthies, such as Pushkin, Gogol and Ivan Susanin were currently being glorified in print. Certain of Kharms's miniatures seem strangely anticipatory of more modern trends: 'The Lecture', in which a man is battered into

unconsciousness as he makes a sexist speech) could almost have
been set now in politically correct America; 'Myshin's Triumph'
smacks of London's cardboard city; while the extract entitled 'On
an Approach to Immortality' would fascinate Kundera.

The most striking feature, for many readers, will be the recur-
rence of Kharms's strange and disturbing obsessions: with falling,
accidents, chance, sudden death, victimization and all forms of
apparently mindless violence. These again are often carried to
extremes, or toyed with in a bizarre manner scarcely uninten-
tional. Frequently there appears little or no difference between
Kharms's avowedly fictional works and his other writings. In his
notebooks can be found such passages as:

> I don't like children, old men, old women, and the rea-
> sonable middle aged. To poison children, that would be
> harsh. But, hell, something needs to be done with
> them!...
>
> I respect only young, robust and splendiferous
> women. The remaining representatives of the human
> race I regard suspiciously. Old women who are reposito-
> ries of reasonable ideas ought to be lassoed...
>
> Which is the more agreeable sight: an old woman
> clad in just a shift, or a young man completely naked?
> And which, in that state, is the less permissible in
> public?...
>
> What's so great about flowers? You get a significantly
> better smell from between women's legs. Both are pure
> nature, so no one dare be outraged at my words.

How far into the cheek the tongue may go is often far from clear:
the degree of identification with narratorial position in Kharms
is always problematic. The better known Kharmsian obsessions,
too (such as falling), carry over into his notebooks and diaries:

On falling into filth, there is only one thing for a man to
do: just fall, without looking round. The important thing
is just to do this with style and energy.

At times the implications might seem particularly sinister, as in
the following note from 1940, which could equally be a sketch for
a story, or even, as we have seen, count as a 'mini-story' in itself:

One man was pursuing another when the latter, who was
running away, in his turn, pursued a third man who, not
sensing the chase behind him, was simply walking at a
brisk pace along the pavement.

Sometimes a diary entry is indeed all but indistinguishable from
a known Kharms miniature:

I used to know a certain watchman who was interested
only in vices. Then his interests narrowed and he began
to be interested only in one vice. And so, when he discovered a specialization of his own within this vice and
began to interest himself only in this one specialization,
he felt himself a man again. Confidence sprang up, eru-
dition was required, neighbouring fields had to be looked
into and the man started to develop. This watchman
became a genius.

Other entries rather more predictably affirm what might be supposed to be his philosophy:

I am interested only in 'nonsense' [*chush'*]; only in that
which makes no practical sense. I am interested in life
only in its absurd manifestation.

This last, apparently frivolous, remark was written in 1937, at the height of the purges.

Some or all of this may be approachable, or even explicable, in terms of psychology, of communication theory, of theory of humour, or indeed with reference to the nature of surrounding reality: in times of extremity, it is the times themselves which seem more absurd than any absurd artistic invention. For that matter, these Kharmsian 'incidents' (on which term, more below) have their ancestry in a multitude of genres and models: the fable, the parable, the fairy tale, the children's story, the philosophical or dramatic dialogue, the comic monologue, carnival, the cartoon and the silent movie. All of these seem to be present somewhere in Kharms, in compressed form and devoid of explanation, context and other standard trappings. Kharms, indeed, seems to serve up, transform or abort, as the case may be, the bare bones of the sub-plots, plot segments and timeless authorial devices of world literature, from the narratives of antiquity, to classic European fiction, to the word-play, plot-play and meta-fictions characteristic of the postmodern era: from *Satyricon* to Cervantes to Calvino. In the modern idiom, theatre of the absurd and theatre of cruelty apart, Kharms's fictions anticipate in some primeval way almost everything from the animated screenplay and the strip cartoon to the video-nasty. Kharms offers a skeletal terseness, as opposed to the comprehensive vacuousness on offer from many a more conventional literary form.

Once again, it is the environment in which he wrote that is the most striking thing of all. Kharms, the black miniaturist, is an exponent not so much of the modernist 'end of the Word' (in a Joycean sense) as of a postmodernist, minimalist and infantilist 'end of the Story' (in a sense perhaps most analogous to Beckett). Such a trend is usually taken to be a post-war, nuclear-age cultural phenomenon, exemplified by fragmentation, breakdown and the impulse to self-destruct. However, the Holocaust and Hiroshima may well have felt imminent in the Leningrad of the bleak 1930s.

Finally, a word on terminology and arrangement. Many of Kharms's stories, even beyond the cycle of that name, have been dubbed 'incidents'. The slightly wider term 'incidences' could equally be used. Kharms, between 1933 and 1937, engaged on a cycle of short prose pieces which he called *sluchai*. The common Russian noun *sluchay* (masculine, singular) may be translated, according to context, by a variety of English words: case (cf. the Italian translation of Kharms, entitled *Casi*), event, incident, occurrence, opportunity, occasion or chance. Commentators have at times labelled the Kharmsian generic innovation: Mini-stories, Happenings or Cases. 'Mini-stories' is of course descriptive, rather than a translation of *sluchai*, just as, say, 'Black Miniatures' would be interpretative; 'Happenings' and 'Cases', I feel, are open to other possible objections. Hence the term 'Incidents', as employed here (with the slightly broader variant, *Incidences*, used as the overall title). Pieces which had not been given a title by Kharms have generally been called by their first words.

Further Reading

Kharms in English

The Man in the Black Coat: Russia's Literature of the Absurd. Selected Works of Daniil Kharms and Alexander Vvedensky. Edited and translated by George Gibian. Northwestern University Press, 1987.
Daniil Ivanovich Kharms, 'The Old Woman'. Translated by Robert Chandler. *Russian Short Stories from Pushkin to Buida*. Edited by Robert Chandler. Penguin Books, 2005.
OBERIU: An Anthology of Russian Absurdism. Translated by Eugene Ostashevsky, Matvei Yankelevich *et al.* Introduction by Susan Sontag.. Northwestern University Press, 2006.

On Kharms

Shukman, Ann, 'Towards a Poetics of the Absurd: The Prose Writings of Daniil Kharms'. *Discontinuous Discourses in Modern Russian Literature*, edited by Catriona Kelly, Michael Makin and David Shepherd. Macmillan, 1989.
Cornwell, Neil (editor), *Daniil Kharms and the Poetics of the Absurd: Essays and Materials*. Macmillan, 1991.
Jaccard, Jean-Philippe, *Daniil Kharms et la fin de l'avant-garde russe*. Peter Lang, 1991.
Stelleman, Jenny, *Aspects of Dramatic Communication: Action, non-action, interaction: (A.P. Cechov, A. Blok, D. Charms)*. Rodopi, 1992.
Aizlewood, Robin, 'Introduction' to D. Kharms, *Starukha/The Old Woman*, edited by Robin Aizlewood, Bristol Classical Press, 1995.
Brandist, Craig, *Carnival Culture and the Soviet Modernist Novel*. Macmillan, 1996.
Roberts, Graham, *The Last Soviet Avant-Garde: OBERIU - Fact, Fiction, Metafiction*. Cambridge University Press, 1997.
Carrick, Neil, *Daniil Kharms: Theologian of the Absurd*. Birmingham Slavonic Monographs, No. 28, 1998.

Cornwell, Neil, 'The Rudiments of Daniil Kharms: In Further Pursuit of the Red-Haired Man'. *Modern Language Review*, 93:1, 1998.

Milner-Gulland, Robin, '"This Could Have Been Foreseen": Kharms's *The Old Woman (Starukha)* Revisited. A Collective Analysis'. *Neo-Formalist Papers*, edited by Joe Andrew and Robert Reid. Rodopi, 1998.

Tokarev, D.B., *Kurs na kudshee: Absurd kak kategoriia teksta u Daniila Kharmsa i Semiuelia Bekketa* ['On Course for the Worst: The Absurd as a Textual Category in Daniil Kharms and Samuel Beckett'], Novoe literaturnoe obozrenie, 2002.

Wanner, Adrian, *Russian Minimalism: From the Prose Poem to the Anti-Story*. Northwestern University Press, 2003.

Cornwell, Neil, *The absurd in literature*. Manchester University Press, 2006.

See also: the Kharms entries in *Reference Guide to Russian Literature*, edited by Neil Cornwell (Fitzroy Dearborn, 1998), pp. 432-7; plus the entries on Kharms, and on the Absurd ('Prose' and 'Theatre of') in the on-line Literary Encyclopedia: http://www.litencyc.com